MARWAN

Damascus – Berlin – Damascus

MARWAN

Damascus – Berlin – Damascus

Khan-Assad-Basha

Damascus, April 2005

Published on the occasion of the exhibition
Marwan
Damascus – Berlin – Damascus

Curator: Mouna Atassi
Organization: Goethe-Institut Damascus, Manfred Ewel
                      Atassi Gallery, Mouna Atassi
Scenography: Hekmat Shatta
Design and layout: Jason Kassab-Bachi, Berlin
Arabic typesetting: Hassan El-Chami, Berlin
Assistant to Marwan: Saïd Baalbaki
Photos: Jörg P. Anders, Jochen Littkemann,
                      Roman März, Marwan,
                      Mohammad Al-Roumi
Additional photos: Jason Kassab-Bachi, Jörn Merkert,
                      Gerd Milting, Anja Möhring,
                      Jonas von Schwedes
Print and repro: Ruksaldruck, Berlin
© Marwan and the authors

With the support
of the European Commission Delegation to Syria.

Acknowledgements to:
The Syrian Ministry of Culture, Dr. Mahmoud al-Sayed
The Syrian Ministry of Expatriates, Dr. Bouthaina Shaaban;
Syrian Embassy Berlin, the Ambassador Dr. Hussein Omran;
Solidere and Nasser Chammaa, Beirut

ATASSI GALLERY

GOETHE-INSTITUT

Marwan and Damascus

After nearly 50 years of having lived and worked in Berlin, and after the creation of a remarkable œuvre, the Syrian born painter Marwan still has to be discovered by the public in his home country. His paintings have been exhibited by numerous museums and galeries throughout Europe, in Egypt, Jordan and Palestine, but until now a representative exhibition in Syria and Lebanon has been missing. Thanks to the efforts of Atassi Gallery, some of his works could be seen in Damascus in 1996, but it is only now that the public in his home town can study his major works in one of the city's best known historic venues.

In cooperation with Atassi Gallery and the Syrian Ministry of Culture, the Goethe-Institut has the honour of presenting Marwan in his many artistic and human aspects: Even from his home in Berlin, Marwan has always been in close contact with outstanding Arab poets or novelists. His work as a painter and graphic artist as well as his long years of teaching at the Berlin Academy of Arts have always benefitted from his sensibility to the memories, colours and poetic sounds of his home country.

This is why we have decided to present not only some of his major works from different periods, but also to invite a group of Marwan's life-time friends to pay hommage to his achievements as an artist and a creative human being. In his paintings as well as in his teachings, Marwan has encouraged many sensitive people to discover the essence of visual art, as well as the possibility of understanding it, even across geographic distance or different cultural backgrounds.

Finally, the organizers of these events would like to acknowledge their thanks to the European Union and all other sponsors for their valuable support in presenting this event to artists and admirers of the arts in Damascus.

Manfred Ewel
Director Goethe-Institut Damascus

Introduction

Can anything more be said about Marwan?
I think not.

The man I know, cannot find solace in words after today, only in that place, the address of which he has lost, the moment he left it.

From that place, Marwan hauled a bundle of dreams, drawing tools, the sapling of a nostalgia, the key to a home, and unburdened (expunged, absolved) himself in a district of the north.

There, he relished in his dreams, reverie followed reverie, for nearly half a century, with the childlike selfishness of the infant who refuses to be weaned.

There, he laid out his tools, unleashed his colours, worked his brushes, garnered exaltation and earned distinction,

There, in the chill of long grey nights, from beneath the comforts of a self absorbed in its selfness, the seedling of nostalgia sprang and yearning wilted,

And there, finally, where estrangement denies permanence, and there are no keys to providence, and myrtle is without aroma, from the garden of his prodigy, the daisies of his craft, and the expanse of a lifetime, Marwan collected a bouquet and offered it to the one he never left for a single day, the one who never left him for a single second: Damascus.

Mouna Atassi
Atassi Gallery, curator   Translation: Racha Salti

5

Jörn Merkert

A Stranger in the World
or, Images for the Thirsty
About Marwan

Strange
is the stranger
only among strangers
Karl Valentin

Enchantment

Marwan's image world has been a continual source of enchantment to me during the past 25 years. It has always seemed at once strange and familiar. In the sense of Ernst Bloch's "daydream of a concrete Utopia" it holds a promising foreignness, a magic that envelops the viewer both directly and imperceptibly. For as much as Marwan's art appears in the sumptuous guise of European painting, it does nothing to conceal its hitherto unseen content. It has its own particular musicality, full of bold, sensuous, rarely heard tone colours. It has an aroma about it that is not of the Occidental world. It conveys a yearning, a quiet, happy melancholy, a deep pain, a cheerful heart – and does so without a trace of literary romancing, but purely through its vividness of colour and form. It is equally of the senses and of the spirit. The viewer coming to Marwan's paintings for the first time thus responds at a very deep level, and the first spontaneous impressions immediately give rise to the question of the work's origins and intentions. And the cheapest way of depriving it of its precious mystique would be to refer to the origins of its creator in the deserts and oases, the gardens and bazaars of Damascus.

But no, his biography will concern us later. At present it would only be the key to the antechamber of the mystery contained within Marwan's art. Becoming unconditionally involved in Marwan's images means entering into an instinctive and unexpectedly intimate dialogue. This can startle now and then, as we are not necessarily prepared for such a thing when encountering works of art. At the very

Postcard showing Mosque Snaniyaha
Bab Al-Jabyeh, 1934

least we are surprised, before his paintings, to find ourselves carrying on a lonely conversation – be it unwanted or unconscious – about ourselves. At first, without any foreknowledge, a curiously moving foreignness in Marwan's work tells us of loss and of lack, of lack too in ourselves. For the yearning revealed in his paintings is not solely the artist's own; everyone carries it within them, and is moved in the reminiscence. Nevertheless this remembered hope for a different or better life is, by its very nature, sited differently in each individual, and is at the same time an individual oasis for the thirsty. Art – always Utopian, i.e. truthful, in dimension – reminds us here of the thirst we all have for the past and future, and also enables us to recognise that the present is not yet a place of fulfilment. Art always reminds us of the lost paradise, but preserves it for us as a treasure – as a promise that on our journey through life becomes a duty.

The wonder is – and here we find a first reliable guide through this alien world – that although Marwan has obviously travelled very widely in his artistic wanderings of almost fifty years, he has always remained entirely true to himself. Even when he seemed to be losing his way, not knowing his path, when the deserts were wide and the oases rare – even then a pattern can be discerned, which to the artist may at times have seemed muddled, but in retrospect always proved to be part of a greater, more far-reaching, meaningful order. This creates trust in oneself, even in despair, and although it may not sooth the most pressing unease, it encourages the taking of new departures. It is as if Marwan had known all along the truth of Bloch's apparently simple maxim: "I am. But I do not have myself. By this we eventually become."[1] But this is a European interpretation and probably does not do justice to the issue of foreignness.

Nevertheless, what Marwan paints – and of course how he paints it – shows the degree to which he has always remained true to himself, this "I am," and the hunger and thirst with which he continues his never-ending search, this "But I do not have myself." And how he recognised early on that there is no fixed goal and no final place, but that we carry within us our own living home – which perhaps we only reach through extensive inner growth – that hopeful yet binding promise, "By this we eventually become." Not alone, but in dialogue with "You, the world," as Paul Klee put it. Or with that consciousness that we are, within the span of birth and death, an inseparable and necessary part of creation.

Marwan paints human images, entirely from within the atmosphere of the moment, again and again, inexhaustible images, with a vividness and depth in which also the unspeakable can be said and the hitherto unseen reveals itself. There are a few still lives, but only a few. They are keenly imbued with sensuous appropriation, and in

1 Ernst Bloch, Tübinger Einleitung in die Philosophie I, Frankfurt 1968,

p. 11, English translation from Rainer E. Zimmermann, The Philosophy of Ernst Bloch, Internet article.

this way effect a vivification of apparently immobile reality. Thus a lifeless marionette, endowed with feelings through the act of painting, becomes a human image. This counterpart to the self – once again, "You, the world" – is then as tempting and consoling, as provocative, coquette, charming, yearning, as rejecting and embracing, as raptly and broodily listening within – and as fearfully, tentatively and joyfully fulfilled – as one's own self on turning to this "You".

Marwan painted only a very few landscapes – occasionally with figures – early on, during his youth in and around Damascus. Later he no longer needed them. Not only because he carries these images within him, and not because the landscapes of his youth – and of the Orient in general – are so precious to him that he does not dare touch on the memory. No, he does not need to paint any more landscapes since he has been able to capture as a matter of course all the sensuous experience of nature in his human images – and not only in his "Facial Landscapes".

The human being, the silent life of things, the inner landscape – Marwan's artistic cosmos consists of these few familiar and quite simple themes. But what is seemingly few is in reality all-encompassing and of as inexhaustible a variety as nature itself, as endlessly broad and as troublingly dense as the landscape, touched by the eternal moment – and particularly so during the past two decades, in which his three great themes have become almost exclusively concentrated on the "Head" pictures, on these landscapes of the soul.

To this day Marwan has remained a stranger in the world. Certainly not only because he emigrated from the Orient to make his life in the Occident. Foreignness is everyone's mystery, for through it we comprehend life. But for Marwan foreignness is not only existentially determined, but is also the vanishing point of desire. It is precisely from a distance that the familiar becomes painfully and delectably foreign. Marwan lives this foreignness and all his paintings tell of it. Foreignness is the door to everything, as it is always a matter of crossing boundaries. The overcoming of foreignness is happiness, is an unveiling and a search for the truth. But one cannot always be near to things, and renewed distance reinstates the foreignness, although one now knows more. Distance is now a veil concealing a mystery that we know and which arouses a sense of longing. This swing of the emotional pendulum, these experiences of nearness and distance, hope and fulfilment, painful loss and happy recollection, seeking and finding, this ceaseless shuttle back and forth, this constantly repeating movement within our lives of mind and heart, is magically translated in Marwan's painting into a direct vividness.

Meeting

I got to know Marwan before we actually met. It must have been 1970 when Werner Haftmann, the former director of the National-galerie, integrated into a re-hanging two curious watercolours. As if in a distorting mirror they showed faces stretched out wide, brown in brown, a little ochre, some yellow perhaps. I didn't want to have seen any other colours; I simply didn't allow myself to be touched. More correctly, on no account did I want to allow myself be moved. Full of youthful prejudice, entirely contemporary, my head and eyes full of pop art, happenings and Fluxus, I was taken aback by the works of this Syrian in Berlin. I felt them to be in the wrong place at the wrong time; for me they were deeply old-fashioned. Even Haftmann, my revered and honoured teacher, could not open my eyes to the fact that they were anything other than conventional in their traditional technique. Another painting joined them a little later, another "Facial Landscape" from 1972. I remained blind, and withdrew; I closed my-self off from something that doubtless had already moved me, as it remained strong in my memory. Yet I did not delve into the particular experience I had involuntarily and spontaneously rejected, as if a dan-ger threatened, as if someone was coming to close, unbidden.

I have seen it frequently in others, and it still applies today: people encountering Marwan's paintings for the first time often close them-selves off defensively – or succumb. For with these works you cannot remain uninvolved and half-hearted. But if you truly open yourself to them they penetrate the soul. Prejudices, particularly when armed with youthful arrogance and relative inexperience, can be persistent and unwavering, for they are needed to hide insecurity, uncertainty and ignorance. It was not until 1975 that I visited him – I was 28 – bringing my scepticism and prejudices with me.[2] It was in his studio in Schmargendorfer Straße.

When I left, after who knows how many hours had passed like a moment, I was truly enchanted. Yet the studio had nothing particu-larly exciting about it. Marwan welcomed me and offered me tea. Tea comes first, to this day. And then he simply showed me his pictures in the wide, initially empty room. I remember our conversation as slow and hesitant at first – but there was also much eloquent silence in looking. He didn't show the paintings in the way I was used to, one after another, leaning up against the wall or hung. No, Marwan placed them – and this is still his method – carefully within the space, supported at only one point by a table or chair. Then comes another, and another, each lightly touching its neighbour, to create a fragilely balanced panorama of images fanning through the room. And if there is time, and if you can't see enough, a second or even third row is added. I finally stood amongst the paintings as if in a garden of count-

Untitled, 1967
Watercolour on paper 62 x 48 cm
Collection of Kupferstichkabinett, Berlin

2 I "only" went to him – as I did to all the other artists Werner Haftmann had supported during his all too short seven years at the Nationalgalerie – to beg for a gift to the museum in honour of its director.

Jörn Merkert and Marwan 2002. Lapidarium, Berlin

less flowers; I was quite still, and felt reminded of Kleist: "As if one's eyelids had been cut away."

The effect of this fragile presentation is that the paintings are experienced as particularly precious, for they do in fact make an appearance – as if for only a moment. They can't stand up like that for long (thinks the inexperienced studio visitor), always in danger of falling over and getting damaged. I didn't understand, that first time – but experienced intensely nonetheless – that this method of presentation exactly corresponds to the content, form and character of Marwan's image world. For the paintings themselves are indeed like apparitions. They are quite ephemeral and vulnerable in the swift notation of their equally fleeting and careful brushwork, and the viewer is attuned to the tenderness they contain, as this is matched by their handling. The images hold something temporal and transitory; the viewer needs time to get into them. But as soon as comprehension occurs they withdraw elusively into quite open, loosely or hardly connected traces of painting, and the singular, even pressing nearness of the faces and figures thus depicted is additionally heightened.

Despite all concentration, the studio visitor is subtly urged into a fluctuating, hasty, almost cursory, subliminal form of looking. And when at times a sheer profusion of painterly events tumbles out of these quiet images, the eye is driven by a certain unease from painting to painting, wanting to take in everything at once, to entirely absorb them, to look its fill and to quench its thirst for colour.

In 1973 Marwan lived for a year in Paris on a scholarship from the Cité des Arts. Here his painting took a bold turn under the overpowering influence of Cézanne, Monet and Manet, of Courbet and Soutine. I did not know then that for Marwan 1973 had been the momentous fulfilment of a youthful dream But let us take the opportunity of following the stages in the development of Marwan's painting this spiritual and sensuous adventure in a more or less ordered review.

Early Departure

In his extensive Arabic monograph on the artist, Abdel Rachman Munif has Marwan relate his childhood and youth in Damascus with such intelligence and vividness that Western ears too can understand that this world has been lost forever.[3] Munif, also telling something of his own story, writes in such a way that the narration, although it remains anchored in the naturalness of the everyday, feels like a wonderful fairytale, imbued with the overpowering aroma of flowers, fruits and spices. Everything gleams in a shimmering light, in the bright colours of the gardens, bazaars and clothing; everything is imbued with the soft, far-off sounds of a bygone age: here the cry of a carter or water seller, the call of the muezzin, there the rattling of a

Marwan 1939

3 Abdel Rachman Munif, Rehlat al Hayad w'al Fan, Damascus 1998, p. 12-19.

Abdelrahman Munif and Marwan 1999 in Damascus

barrow, the splash of a fountain, the song of a bird, a high-pitched laugh, the clatter of horses' hooves on the roads, more muffled under trees and silent in the sands of the desert – Marwan's world. But it has not only vanished, in the way every childhood becomes a dream; the loss is greater, much greater, for the world Munif relates has been submerged by the political confusion of the Middle East, and the old Syria almost crushed between the burden of history and the destructiveness of the modern era. Yet the ancient dream of the holy city of – even then – times long past is still held true in people's consciousness: "By Allah, they spoke the truth who said that if there were a paradise on earth it were without doubt Damascus; and if it were in heaven, then Damascus were its earthly counterpart," wrote the Andalusian traveller Ibn Jubayr on 5 July 1184[4] about this thousand-year-old melting pot of peoples and languages, cultures and religions.

Marwan has been able to preserve a whole series of paintings from his youth. Aside from portraits of his sister they are above all landscapes. To the Western eye they show an astonishing confidence and freshness along with the understandable awkwardness of the early attempt and much atmosphere, which is captured in lively, open brushstrokes. As if Marwan had already seen impressionist paintings, or knew the fragmentary style of Cézanne's unfinished pictures or the shimmering transparency of certain works of Bonnard or Vuillard. He may have seen them in Western books or art journals, although scarcely in colour reproductions, and if so, then ones of poor quality. But how much easier it must have been for this boy to project and dream into these reproductions the colours of his own world and thus to awaken a yearning to see the originals in all their glory, and one day even to be able to paint as wonderfully himself. The longing for Europe, for this alien world, was stirred, and the dream was Paris.

Marwan never seems to have doubted that he would become a painter – that he would follow a career that does not really exist in the Arab world, and for which in Syria at that time there was as good as no professional training. Against this background it is astonishing to see how well he prepared himself for his spiritual journey and his departure for the West. For very soon his painting takes an unexpected and completely different turn – obviously influenced by 20th-century European work, the originals of which he also could not have

4 Translated from Johannes Odenthal, Syrien Hochkulturen zwischen Mittelmeer und Arabischer Wüste, DuMont Kunst-Reiseführer, Cologne 1995, p.70.

Landscape near Damascus 1953,
Oil on canvas, 39 x 30 cm

seen. Where only a short while before his subject matter had been the lifelike, atmospheric depiction of the landscape, the paint dabbed on with a few brushstrokes, suddenly the surface of the paintings is exactly what in reality it actually is: flat. The architecture of the image is made up of a few extended fields of colour placed alongside or opposite one another as if cut out. The simply and clearly ordered colouring of Matisse cannot be overlooked.

But in a work like "The Pitcher", painted in 1956 when Marwan was 22, he has entirely captured his Middle Eastern world in this Western visual language. Brown and ochre are of course – quite materially and thus almost naturalistically – the condensing into colour of desert and stone and fertile earth. Furrowed by circular movement, the colours fill the entire surface. Space is no longer depicted; everything is flat – as if a hand has brushed through the sandy ground. This close-up view, without a horizon, at the same time depicts the breath-taking, immeasurable expanse of the landscape. And those who live there need little, although what they do need is indispensable: the earthen pitcher, symbolising with its arabesque, curving handle and spout the bubbling flow of precious water; the lemon, embodiment of refreshment, that delicious fruit wrung from the barren ground with hard work and God's help. And then the eye, the Eye of Fatima that protects against evil. Allah is near and within everything.

At 23 Marwan painted a picture that can be seen to prefigure what was to come. It shows the rear view of a yellow girl, her long black hair drawn into a severe braid that vertically divides her back.

The Pitcher, 1956
Oil on canvas, 34 x 43,5 cm

She sits on a black stone in a starry, anthracite night. That is all. A dream image. An image of human longing. The heat of the day has caught itself up in the girl's body like a constant blinding glow; the night is cooling. Everything is clothed in mystery, for the image shows nothing. The girl sits turned away, sunk within herself – we are observers projecting our own dreams onto her. Once again we see the strict, entirely free, flat painterly colour-architecture that we know from Matisse. Yet once again it is all authentically imbued with impressions from the far-off, to us foreign, Arab world

– even though we are scarcely able to say how Marwan does it. The European – how could it be otherwise? – naturally thinks of Caspar David Friedrich's repoussoir figures, which draw the gaze into the painted space. But in his paintings – in the European spirit – longing is attached to an object, such as the symbolic ship, whereas in Marwan's image it is absorbed into the blackness of the firmament, as abstract as Islam itself, that religion of the word.

It is different in the painting "Two Friends", in which cipher-like notations on a dark background – a bird in a tree, a small flock of birds in the night sky, a sailing boat on a calm lake – softly evoke the two women's peaceful harmony with nature, as if in a miniature from an old illuminated manuscript. But ambivalence and mystery are here too. If the one – with her glowing cheeks and curving open lips – seems flooded with the ardent longing of a blossoming desire, the other – with her pale yellow face – stands for the omnipresence of death, which embraces us in the midst of life. The scene is framed by a delicate pattern of yellow lines, like a gateway, a window – a bordering world – that distantly reminds one of the glittering gold mosaics of certain mosques.

Berlin, 1958

If the subject matter of both paintings is painful longing, hopeful anticipation and human loneliness, these atmospheres are above all carried by a harmony with the surrounding world. It is a harmony with oneself which, although bearing witness to an integral identity – "I am" – is not in possession of the world. It is already touched by a first, gnawing sense of inadequacy – "But I do not have myself." And in this lightly fissured harmony Marwan does now turn towards his departure. Setting out to satisfy his longing for the colours of the north and the great painters of that foreign world, he exchanges it for the more painful yearning for the "oriental twilight, at the edge of the Syrian steppes, with its silky orange, violet and emerald green."[5] And for this reason among others this "I am" will soon, for several years, appear to be entirely lost, and very little will remain of that hopeful atmosphere of departure into one's future – of "becoming."

5 From the text of Marwan's invitation to his 65th birthday on 31 January 1999.

Fear Eats the Soul

It would take a while before he actually reached Paris. In September of 1957 – after a long sea journey to Genoa, and via a detour through Munich – he arrived, more or less by chance – in Berlin, the city still lying desolate, marked by destruction, bomb craters and fields of rubble. In the class of his teacher Hann Trier at the College of Visual Arts he found German art informel, American abstract impressionism, French abstraction lyrique and tachisme. As a stylistic direction, and in the attitude to the world it expressed, this global artistic language determined everything at that time. It influenced the way artists saw themselves, gave rise to a concept of the image as open and fragmentary and encouraged a high degree of poetic license in regard to the realities of the world captured in these abstract works.

In its spontaneous protocol of gesticulatory markings, and solely through autonomous painterly means, this type of painting endeavoured to create a sensual response to the invisible inner world. An uncontrolled painterly dynamic and a hot-and-cold tension in the use of colour were intended to translate into resounding visuality an unsparing psychograph of artistic existence, with its unplumbed depths and almost unnameable emotions – an idea of the image as entirely immaterial. This required of Marwan a radical break with his previous image world – and much hard work – and may even have been accompanied by disappointment at no longer having the means to give touching clarity to his feeling for life. But he learned how to understand colour more exactly as a value in itself, to allow it its own life while mastering it step by step, to discover its autonomous expressive language, independent of the world of objects, and to research the spatially suggestive power of colouristic constellation. The nuanced attitude to colour would later become the backbone of his painting – that was the hope. Damascus was not forgotten, but unreachably distant. He earned his living as a furrier's assistant, and generally painted at night.

Marwan has only preserved a few of his paintings from this time. At around 1960 he had for the moment acquired a steady foundation. Strictly limited to a few colours – mainly black, white and grey tones, sometimes shimmering mother-of-pearl – his images have an exceptional painterly compression, as if something physical is urging its manifestation on the canvas. Space – or, more exactly, visual plasticity – is developed entirely through the overlaying and interweaving of colour. There is no perspective, no depiction – and yet there is an almost desirous carnality, and always an intimation of landscape.

And very soon there is a distinct sense of lack, of the inadequacy of the abstract image, of Marwan's unsatisfied hunger for the tangible vividness of poetically heightened depiction. It was the same for some of his fellow students. At first there was the familiar youthful refusal to imitate the fathers, and thus to seek mastery in an opposite field. But then there were other and to Marwan alien, very German reasons. In 1961 and 1962 Eugen Schönebeck and Georg Baselitz sent an expressive, staccato outpouring of suffering into the world with their now legendary, jointly authored Pandemonic Manifesto, which articulated with the poetic backing of Artaud and Lautréamont the mood of an entire generation. A generation that saw itself in tragic terms, burdened with the weight of German history and conscious of the responsibility of remembering and reawakening the nightmares of

Untitled, 1960
Oil on canvas, 120 x 100 cm

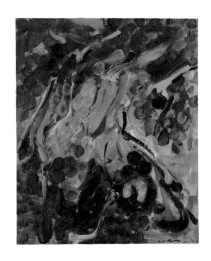

their parents. In their eyes abstract painting seemed unsuited to the task of creating the counter-images required[6] – despite the example of those such as Wols, or of Fautrier's political "Otages" series.

In his personal search for a new figurative painting this of course was not Marwan's impetus. As a "lost individual" he carried something quite different within him – a painful tension of the soul demanding authentic expression, dissolution, understanding, ease. He must have felt an icy loneliness during these years, filled with a longing for affection, security and belonging.

Marwan was part of the circle of artists around Schönebeck and Baselitz. He took part in their discussions, came to understand an obviously parallel if quite differently weighted and foreign form of disaffection with the world and encountered a related poetic eye yet in his language and cultural consciousness he stood quite outside this circle.

An example of this groping, transitional search between the worlds of abstraction and figurativeness, that for him were so differ-

6 See Jörn Merkert, Laudatio auf Eugen Schönebeck, Festschrift für den Fred Thieler Preis für Malerei 1992, Berlinische Galerie, Berlin 1992, p. 4-14.

Figuration, 1963 / 64
Oil on canvas, 89 x 130 cm
Collection Berlinische Galerie, Berlin

ently rooted culturally, is "Figuration", of 1963/64, whose figures can barely be deciphered. But the image awakens sombre associations. To understand it one needs to recall the yellow girl with the black braid. We find the same topos: a nocturnal horizon, now with a reclining figure. But the sky is no longer bedecked with stars; it is burdensome and impenetrable. And the figure – painted in the abstract-psychological manner of tachisme – is a muddled pile of raw flesh: two entwined human bodies, even, torn limb from limb? Everything is ambivalent, held in an echoing silence. It is the epitome of destruction, suffering, injury and mortality – and in its deep nocturnal darkness it reminds one from afar of the black paintings of the deaf Goya. "Untitled" of 1964 takes up the same subject matter in apparently more concrete terms. The bloody mountain of torn flesh now vaguely evokes an organic form with widely gaping jaws – a stranded, all-devouring leviathan. Above it a mythical figure hovers threateningly in the dusky gloom.

Considering what was still to come in Marwan's image world, two things should be remembered here: first, that the lively, intensely animated yet differentiated, purely abstract mode of painting is restricted to the nightmarish bodies, which have devoured everything living, literally and visibly carrying it within them. The remaining scenery, in contrast, with its silver dawn on a far horizon and the black remains of the night above, is quite still, painted tone in tone in quiet, subdued colours without any sign of life. Content – paralysing emptiness and wild, animalistic greed – is congruent here with its mode of painting. The second thing is the unusual form of composition, which Marwan will not take up again for decades, but which bears the seed of a later, surprising visual discovery: the division of the image into two for the purpose of a double depiction – like a reflection. And, despite the landscape theme, Marwan characteristically succeeds in retaining his clear, flat visual architecture – still distantly related to Matisse – in an entirely transformed guise.

In the mid 1960s his path becomes clearer, and so do his paintings. In the extensive cycle depicting human forms, individual figures and couples now face the viewer in unsparing, challenging directness. They all stand in an oppressively empty space, from which the outside world has entirely vanished, and are all in such dire straits that their

Figuration, 1966
Oil on canvas, 195 x 130 cm

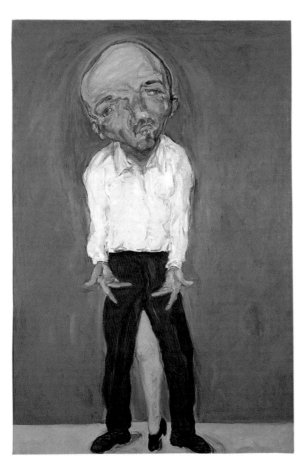

bodies, and particularly their faces, are deformed, as if under pressure. They are mute, as if hermetically sealed by a glass wall. They seem enclosed in silence, which they attempt to break with an aggressive sign language bordering on the obscene[7] Surreal disturbances are inserted into the images in the form of a second, fragmented figure, as if hidden by the first – bodiless arms embrace the hips; the naked leg of an otherwise invisible figure appears between those of a man; a hand emerging from the numinous background sticks its finger into an eye. But there is no narrative. The figures persist in their silent outcry, even if they are not alone. Worlds lie between these couples and the "Two Friends" painted ten years earlier in Damascus.

But we should not deceive ourselves. Although this cycle of work contains the most self-portraits in the representational sense – although they are no less "surreal" than the other paintings – these human images, wrung painfully from reality with hallucinatory clairvoyance, are not at all simply the individualistic interpretations of a lost and foreign loner. "They concentrate and focus the psychological

7 See my detailed analysis of this workgroup in Jörn Merkert, Marwans unbekanntes Frühwerk, in the exhibition catalogue Marwan Frühe Aquarelle, Galerie Michael Hasenclever, Munich 1990.

Facial Landscape, 1973
Pastel on canvas, 162 x 228 cm
Collection Berlinische Galerie, Berlin

8 ibid.

9 "pathetische Figuration", Eberhard Roters, foreword to the
exhibition catalogue Marwan, Galerie Springer, Berlin 1967,
p. 20-21.

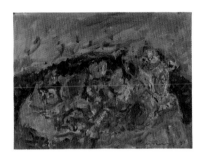

Stillife, 1981
Oil on canvas, 60 x 81 cm

state of a society by making ironic use of exactly the absurdity and
apparent unreality this society embodies"[8] – and are thus related to
those "absurd" human images that Samuel Beckett or Edward Albee
were putting on stage at the time.

Gift and Fulfilment

Around 1970, Marwan was able to calm the disturbed, traumatised
world of his "melodramatic figuration."[9] In his "Facial Landscapes",
he zooms in like a film camera on his forms, whose tormented inner
world is thus revealed. The facial close-up alone is the intimate subject
matter of the paintings. And this visual closeness is also a literal affection and closeness that allows the longings, joys and hopes engraved
in these faces to appear undisguised. The terrible emotional wounds
of the previous works seem almost to have been washed away by this
tenderly cautious and touching nearness.

Having observed how Marwan, in the images with the mythical
creatures, placed his painterly expressiveness in the formation of the
bodies, we can see a similar tendency in the pictures of human figures.
In contrast to the paralysing, silent vortex of the interior, the heightened vivification his painting achieves is entirely concentrated on the
figure, and above all on the face. Now, in the "Facial Landscapes",
with flowing brushwork and a soft, tender colouration, he allows
himself – as if liberated – an extraordinarily nuanced, expressive, pul-
sating and emotional language. The subject matter is also a means
of further developing his painting. And it is anything other than by
chance that Marwan once again recalls the variety and expressive
power of the abstract, gesticulatory colouring of the art informel of
his student days. Carefully and cautiously, yet with obviously clear
intentions, he makes use of colour in a way that is quite removed
from all figurative associations in order to let the depiction emerge
from within the qualities of the paint itself. He varnishes, overpaints,
allows the broken brown tones to flow into one another, very occasionally heightening with white or a clear primary colour. Everything
shimmers, is flooded with light; there are hardly any fixed contours.
As if floating, the colours weave themselves into a silky consistency.
And this is why these faces are also landscapes – landscapes of the
soul and of the mind. But, surprisingly, they are also landscapes of
dreamlike memory. In almost every painting the great soaring skull
of the horizon also reminds one distantly and unexpectedly of the
Qassyun towering above Damascus, when at dusk, after the heat of
the day, a gentle breeze flutters over the city lights, bringing with it the
scent of the awakening night, and happiness is so very near.
If in the series of human figures Marwan had often painted obvi-
ous self-portraits – and if others from this group could vaguely be

identified as his own likeness in the expressive excess of their depiction – in the "Facial Landscapes" everything begins to interpenetrate – free portrayal and authentic portrait. At times the outer similarity disappears entirely in favour of a form of representation that follows only the autonomous law of the image and the precision of painterly expression. And yet the viewer always feels that these pictures are a true likeness of Marwan, of his inner world. The portrayal no longer requires outer similarity, but is – on a completely different, mental-emotional level – the epitome of the self. The image is here to a certain extent already quite abstract, which is why there is no necessity for wanting to recognise Marwan's portrait in them. In the transformation through painting, these images gain a universality beyond any attachment to the individuality of the person portrayed.

Marwan was obviously well prepared for the second great formative departure of his life. In 1973 he received a scholarship for the Cité des Arts and was able to realise the long-held dream of his youth. In Paris colour is returned to him the colour he had brought with him as a precious memory from the edge of the Syrian steppes, yet had not yet really dared to use, that silky orange, violet and emerald green.

The Veil, 1973
Oil on canvas, 130 x 195 cm

For remembering them with longing is quite a different matter from being able to paint them.

But the encounter with French impressionism – so easily held to be a mere stylistic direction – and then with the old masters – such as Velazquez, whom Marwan much admired – and finally with Western 20th-century modernism, freed him from any inhibition about joining the feast of colour. His paintings now take on a cheerful musicality in a free, dancing notation of generally pure colour.

In his "Veil Paintings" he quite directly takes up the theme of concealment and revelation mentioned at the start of this article. Here in Paris it gains an almost Mozartian cheerfulness and wisdom. The images come out to meet the viewer in an urgent, suggestive plasticity; they demand a dialogue. Bedecked in light veils, they tempt – often in androgynous ambivalence – and withdraw in an alternating game of attraction and evasion. Longing for the entirely other – longing indeed based in otherness – is here bathed in soft addictive colour.

In Paris the Facial Landscapes and the Veil Paintings coalesce into the first of the Heads, that in the coming years and decades will become Marwan's almost sole theme. The treasure trove of freely used colour was brought back to Berlin, to unfold over the following years into a magnificent splendour. Whether painting alongside the Heads his few still lives during the 1970s, or around 1980 the first of the Marionettes, he is always concerned with cultivating the garden of purely abstract, gesticulatory painting in such a way that with it he can translate everything i.e. the unity of world and experience into a pure visual poetry that moves the spirit and senses. The still life is an important instrument in formulating this aim in a more differentiated way. For here the concern is to vivify dead material in such a way that in a piece of fruit, a bowl, a jug as with Cézanne's Natures mortes or Morandi's receptacles the human drama of love and death, longing and fulfilment, hope and mortality is made visible through tangible sensory experience.

Visiting him in his studio, we have already attempted to grasp the characteristic contradiction that although Marwan's paintings posses an extraordinary concentration – i.e. great exactitude in their apparently lightly flowing brushstrokes – the gaze is seduced into what was described above as a form of cursory observation. It is not a superficial form of looking that is meant here, and various aspects of Marwan's art are caught up in it. This way of reading the images exactly corresponds to the way they are created, which is characterised equally by great speed and the need for time. For they are painted over again and again – sometimes after many years, face over face – so that a countenance apparently full of composure contains many others, just as our own is the result of years of transformation. And yet it can alter in expression from moment to moment, showing many faces in one. Marwan's paintings are very real, like life. How long a plant needs before the bud appears, and how quickly it withers! Here we find the central motivating tension in Marwan's art: the attempt, familiar down the ages, to seize the transitory moment and retain it forever. Now we can better understand why Marwan's painting, with its magnificence of colour, encompassing the "silky orange, violet and emerald green of the oriental twilight," is able to preserve all his yearning memories – and why it is so deeply true.

I was able to experience this for myself when in 1996 Marwan began to paint my portrait. Applying his art of lively human portrayal to the task of recognisable depiction was not only a concern of his early self-portraits; it also occupied him during the following decades and did so increasingly so until today. This was the first time I had the opportunity of observing Marwan at work. I was allowed to sit comfortably; we listened to music – Arabian, classical and early music – conversed, even drank tea. But concentration was also required of the model in retaining his posture, although not in every detail. Painting, for Marwan, is of course a physical act; not in applying the paint, but in the back-and-forth of looking, which has not only to do with the eyes. He constantly had to move away from the canvas to obtain an exact impression of a shading, a fall of light, the form of the nose or eyebrows. And then the "right" colour had to be selected – and the table on which his paints lie in veritable piles is in itself a distracting feast for the eyes. A short hesitation, a mixing of tones, another look, no, the colour isn't right, renewed mixing and dabbing – and then the image requires something quite different, is no longer painted at the top, but at the bottom or the side, and for this Marwan needs other colours. It is a wonder that what is seen is not lost again in between looking, mixing and painting. As indeed it sometimes is, and the whole procedure is begun again. Sometimes a small detail will be reworked repeatedly, while another is set at a stroke once and for all. At each break I saw a completely different painting, yet always recognised myself. And at each new sitting – which usually began with doubts as to whether anything should be altered at all – the painting was completely transformed and taken in a new direction. It was a marvel, although coupled

Top: portrait Jörn Merkert, 1996 / 98
Oil on canvas

Bottom: state of the same portrait, 1996
Oil on canvas

with a painful feeling of loss – as the earlier versions would never be seen again. The first portrait – on which he worked in at least seven sittings until 1998 – was at first of a light, transparent appearance and had much magic about it. But it then compressed into an image containing many of my faces simultaneously, most of which I am able to recognise. Other people – some of them good friends – have their difficulties and need time, as they probably know other faces of mine, and perhaps not those known to Marwan. It remains astounding how he is able, despite the similarity contained in the depiction, to remain true to his autonomous painting and to allow the portrayal, from approximation to exactitude, to emerge from it.

But there is something else bound up with this complex temporal contradiction in Marwan's art – something that will also be seen to have deeply human roots – and that is a quality manifest in most of his paintings, and in all the faces and heads. The work addresses the sacred – and yet is also of extreme, even despairing, modernity. We can come to an ideal understanding of this through Giacometti, who in all his sculptures dealt with the very contemporary problem of the abolition of perspective, the cancellation of the very near and the very distant. From far away I see a figure clearly, but no details; from nearby I see every detail exactly, but no longer have the whole picture. But in reality the person Giacometti wishes to portray consists of both these aspects of our perception, and thus there are tiny sculptures that remain in the distance even when near to the viewer, and tall ones revealing a near view even from afar.

Marwan's "Head" paintings are similar. He too paints tiny and giant formats – with the same intensity, the same inexhaustible variety of expression – and the same contradictory simultaneity of proximity and distance. We meet this phenomenon particularly in the heads, which were always portrayed in close-up, and over the years – incredibly – have moved even nearer to the viewer. Because they are in fact not "portrayed", but emerge naturally and spontaneously from a mode of abstract painting, we can only see them with complete clarity when we encounter them from a distance, when the great closeness of expression in the images becomes apparent. As we move towards them, they gradually dissolve and elude our grasp, unfolding instead a shimmering, radiant, flickering, blossoming, fading field of sumptuous individual colourations, every detail of which holds the proximity just experienced. This is also how Marwan is able to depict more than just the person in his paintings, and why all memory, all longing, all despair and all certainty are caught in his sensuous network of colour and the handwriting-like flow of his brushwork. Thus we actually do encounter a coming into possession of the world in the sense of Ernst Bloch: "I am. But I do not have myself. By this we eventually become."

Marwan near the Hicham hunting residence in the desert, Jordan 1998

Between the Worlds

I had the good fortune of accompanying Marwan on a number of his journeys to Damascus and through Syria, to Amman and through Jordan. Despite all the modern, hectic bustle of the cities and their inhabitants, it was often possible to discover traces of Marwan's bygone world, which he carries alive within him, and indeed incarnates. Commenting on one of my texts on Marwan, my old teacher Werner Haftmann once wrote: "That is very authentic: this mild Syrian's response in a European language to what he carries within him – the baroque and the desert, together with the lonely sensuousness of the Bedouin."[10] That captures it exactly, but not only Marwan's image world. For his far-ranging journey through life has and how could it be otherwise? torn him from his biographical home. When he is with the friends and companions of his youth, or with his family, he is welcomed with joy like a long-lost son. But for those of them who know him well he carries something foreign within him. For he is the one who has gone out into the wide world, only to return for short periods. With his mild Bedouin soul he has brought something

10 Letter to the author from Werner Haftmann, 19.1.1977, translated from Jörn Merkert, Kadousch oder die Verwandlung Fragmentarische Überlegungen zu Marwans Bildern, in the exhibition catalogue Marwan, Kunstverein Darmstadt, Verlag für zeitgenössische Kunst, Berlin 1984, p. 19.

The Friend, 2004
Oil on canvas, 89 x 130 cm

Oriental into Western art; he has mastered the language of European art even in the face of its glorious tradition of painting like no other, and yet has steadfastly related the wonders of the world from which he comes. And so he is gratefully admired, while also having become a foreigner. For it is not easy for his Arab friends to recognise in a foreign visual language what is so familiar to them. And amidst the admiration for his work in the Arab world there is scarcely a feeling for the foreignness Marwan experienced within himself in Europe and which Europe at times compels him to experience. In Berlin this is different, of course; and also in Paris, where he is held in high esteem from the Institut du Monde Arabe to the Bibliothèque Nationale. In these cities his foreignness to both worlds is valued.

Marwan has become the master from a strange world, and remained a stranger in the world. He has given us all his marvellous paintings, in which humanity's inherent dreams are exemplified and preserved, enchanting us with a reminiscent, yearning, consoling magic.

Translation: Michael Turnbull

Figuration, 1966
Oil on canvas, 162 x 114 cm

Joachim Sartorius
Speech in Honour of Marwan
Thieler Prize 2002

Jarba Village, 1947 or 48
Oil on wood 13 x 17,9 cm

The first of Marwan's extant paintings shows the landscape before the gates of his home city. Reminiscent of French impressionism, it was painted with confident lightness in Damascus in 1947/48, when the artist was 13. In his studio in Schmargendorfer Straße, a large sombre image of two heads leaning together is currently emerging. We are celebrating today the unwavering journey of almost fifty years of the painter Marwan. What do I mean by "unwavering"? In the half a century from 1947/48 to today, during which time painting has often been beset by other techniques, or indeed given up for dead, Marwan has continually bestowed the medium with new triumphs of emotional imagery clearly differentiated from realistic, abstract, constructivist or installationist art. By "unwavering" I also mean that Marwan – if we attempt an overview of his oeuvre from the early landscapes to the part abstract, part figurative monsters, to the couples, giant heads, melodramatic facial landscapes, marionettes, still lives, once again monumental heads and finally pairs of heads – has always searched for a formal vocabulary that allowed the transformation into painting of existential questions.

"I think utterly existentially," Marwan once told me in his studio, and also that "a painting is like a wound." In his search for images he most probably starts from concrete occurrences, yet his painting is not an art of consternation. He knows too well that poetic language – of which he is a master, and which, for example, his friend the great Syrian poet Adonis finds in human disquiet and suffering – is radically different from visual language. To express loss in an image, to allow pain to appear, to paint the stillness of thousands of years, is a difficult process. Marwan likes to compare the artist with the architect. He needs a long time for a painting. In some years only four or five are "completed", i.e. considered by him to have been truly concluded. He applies layer after layer, with great patience and intensity, as if a crystallisation of experience were taking place. I wanted to express this in a poem, and wrote:

Figuration, 1964
Egg tempera on canvas, 89 x 130 cm

> *"for there is only the face*
> *constructed rejected*
> *set up once again vibrating*
> *from death into life*
> *returning, the indelible countenance"*

Particularly the human images of the past few years – with their thick layers of paint, where blue and green tunnel under deepest red, where yellow breaks out of grey-black craters and broken brown tones interweave and shimmer – bring to my mind the Islamic idea of the origin of humankind: from the earth, from a seed, growing and taking on many forms before its final perfection.

Marwan is a painter above all. The story behind an image, or whatever its starting point might be – the veils of the women in Damascus or the murdered Palestinian in the arms of his friend – is not what he is finally interested in. His painting is concerned with the relationship to one another of surfaces of colour, with layers of colour, with a deft balancing, with a dark glow coming into light, bathing us in its delicacy. Nowhere in contemporary painting can it be more easily seen than in Marwan's work that colours have both physical *and* emotional properties. Even in the comparatively realistic so-called "Figurations" of the late 1960s he was not seeking the depiction, but rather the painterly truth, of his subjects. And, considering the lengthy creative process involved, this also means that a part of his existence has quite physically entered each painting. All his pictures, but particularly those of the past decade, are an emotionally compressed, and thus almost abstract, expression of the suffering of human existence, filled with the burning of pain, the shock of insight and the wounds of love. Compelled to name Marwan's artistic forefathers, I would place Antonin Artaud first, and his unforgettable portraits and self-portraits, created in the asylum at Rodez, which show the same balance between emergence and disintegration that Marwan attempts each day at his easel. Then Edvard Munch and Vincent van Gogh, because of the painterly intelligence and vision of their insight into human existence. Then Alberto Giacometti, because of the collapse of proximity and distance within the portrayal; in Marwan's work too the face, on approaching it, gradually dissolves into a free play of colour. And finally Mark Rothko, who as almost no other was able to express meditation, stillness and reticence. Marwan does not share Rothko's sublimity – his paintings, for all their meditative contemplation, are too aggressive – but his monumental heads at times attain the quality of icons, of the divine countenance, of universality, and are thus – at least in my view – related to Rothko's mysticism. We can experience an almost unbearable stillness of the universe in the work of both artists.

Head, 1996
Oil on canvas, 146 x 195 cm

Many years ago I was witness to a conversation between Heiner Müller and Iannis Kounellis in the Paris Bar. They were discussing what it is that makes great art. Here one should know that Heiner Müller was speaking bad English and good German, Kounellis bad Italian and bad Greek. So the two were gesticulating, laughing, making little drawings on the serviettes and using their fingers and hands, the better to explain and also to hear one another. The result of this remarkable conversation was that "great art" had to combine an international vocabulary with radical subjective and local elements. In Marwan's case the influence of his homeland Syria has often been a focus of inquiry. In ancient times, until well into the Ottoman period, Syria was an open zone of encounter between Persia and Anatolia, Egypt, the Mediterranean and the Levant. Almost the exact opposite of Berlin, the uncomfortable, divided, cold, northern city where Marwan – in the unforgettable phrase of Eberhard Roters – "found his artistic Damascus." The real Damascus of his childhood was a place of security and sensuousness. Marwan can talk very vividly about it: the violet evening light, the kites whirring in the sky, the green light in the courtyards, absorbed by vegetation, the veiled women and how arousing they were for adolescent boys. He can wonderfully evoke the sublimated sensuousness of the Orient that we can also experience in its carpets, its marvellously colourful illuminated manuscripts or in the dark and gold of the mosaics in the Great Mosque of Damascus.

But I must confess that I do not know how much of all this is *concretely* present in Marwan's paintings. From 1955 to 1957 he studied Arabic literature at the University of Damascus. In September 1957 he came to Berlin and became a student of Hann Trier at the *Hochschule der Künste* (College of Art), where he got to grips for a short time with tachisme. During a scholarship to Paris in 1973 he professed to the play of festive colour that had always been within him as his Arab heritage. If the cipher of Damascus is present in his work, then as a spiritual attitude, as an invisible visual structure, as a secret within the brushwork, as transcendence.

So much to the subjective, local and hermetic elements. What about the "internationally comprehensible vocabulary"? There is a constant in Marwan's half a century of art. It is the head – we might also say the face, the countenance. The head as the site of the ultimate questions. The three parts of one of the most important novels of the 20th century, Elias Cannetti's "Auto-da-Fé" are entitled "A Head without a World", "Headless World" and "The World in the Head". Marwan conceives of the head as a world, as a landscape of the soul, as the great orb of the universe. An arena of love and melancholy, because the eyes, with or without pupils, are always turned inwards, at once glowing and rejecting. Marwan has refined this central motif over many decades, and despite its limitation in terms of content it reflects his entire artistic range. It culminates in the series "99 Heads", that incomparable collection of graphic works which may certainly be described as a quintessence of visual invention and technical mastery. As if in a myriad of reflections and visual similes, Marwan meditates here on the basic human state of being, bringing forth deeply valid statements about vulnerability, fear or timidity, but also about self-confidence and unreserved solidarity. The capacity for life of Marwan's heads is continually astounding; they stand for the whole body and thus for the human being.

In this connection we should remember that the head is one of the main themes of 20th-century art. We need only think of the heads of Brancusi, Archipenko, Hans Uhlmann or Horst Antes. The abstract portrait – although in its abstraction never idealised or anonymous – was the result of a long development that started around 1890, when the art of portraiture was released from its mimetic function to concentrate on generalised formulations of the head. This led to the hitherto unimaginable stylisation of the cubist portraits, which radically annulled the imitative requirements of the genre. Such portrayals, including Marwan's later massive heads,

In Bed, 1971

Oil on canvas, 33 x 46 cm

are in the end artistic constructions valid only in the aesthetic realm. But there they are charged with quite a different meaning, which – in Marwan's case – touches the magical and the mystic.

Are we not all searching for a strong metaphor, for an incarnation? Marwan finds his in the head; he finds the world in the head. And so he paints the head not as a matter of preference, but from within a deeper, more passionate desire to display and explain the world. His continual return to the heads from other motifs – from the iridescent still lives, in which objects lead a dramatic life of their own; from the marionettes, the projection surface for a sensuously liberated form of absolute painting – reflects a wish to convey his most concentrated description of the world. He varies and reiterates his motifs; he reiterates the world. If we look at these heads for a long time, letting them into us until they let us in, we enter an intermediate realm, somewhere between archaic stillness and outward sorrow – a silent scream.

Perhaps this is what the American poet Clayton Eshleman wanted to express in his poem about Marwan's "Faces":

> *"... the human face ...*
> *is a kind of rug before its shape*
> *is fixed –*
> *in Marwan's work –*
> *in a between that is not*
> *a mystical point between us*
> *but a depth between the deathmask of the covering*
> *Persona and peeled of skin."*

This "between", which is also a depth, speaks of a tension – we might also say ambivalence or duality – present in all Marwan's work periods. It struck me as an essential quality of his paintings when I saw them for the first time in the Pudelko Gallery in Bonn in 1973. On exhibition were the large "Facial Landscapes": flat heads on cushions, emerging from sheets, some with very transparent veils; strangely isolated, inhibited people with problematic identities. It was as if they had been painted with a soft anger. They swayed between masculine and feminine, between revealing and concealing, between the fear of loneliness and the longing thereafter. And Marwan's paintings carry such ambivalences to this day.

In certain periods of work this duality is inherent to the visual construction. In 1963/64 he painted a number of pictures with two amorphous figures: monsters washed up onto a grey land under a black sky, the atmosphere leaden. This doubling is now reoccurring in large-format images of two faces, one above the other, like reflections in a dividing line of water, or side by side, the one head some-

Head, 1993
Oil on canvas, 195 x 130 cm

The Friend, 2001
Watercolour on paper, 21 x 29,7 cm
from a sketchbook

Opposite:
Reflection, 2004
Oil on canvas, 195 x 114 cm

Translation: Michael Turnbull

times turned away and leaning on its counterpart. Marwan entitles these dual heads "The Friend", which in Arabic is also an expression for death. The head facing us is painted in countless warm tones – dabbings of red, yellow, orange and ochre that set the surface in motion, giving it a rhythm that flows around the other face. This second one is paler, grey and whitish and green; lifeless, in fact, a cipher for death embraced by life. It may be erroneous, but at the sight of these lifeless heads I had to think of Veronica's veil – and of the medieval pietas.

The goal of Marwan's unwavering journey – which was not without its detours and sidetracks and returnings – is the recognition of all that is human. This recognition rejects nihilism. In the imperious, archaic heads of recent years we discern the transformations of a soul that has sought to join with the enigmatic, the unspeakable – perhaps even with the divine.

They are frail, these people. But their weakness – brother to longing – also gives them a strength that can immediately be seen in the frontal countenance, the high forehead, the powerful mouth; a strength that hints at something invincible, as if the person dying in the other is yet reborn. We cannot view the paintings of this most recent period without considering their metaphysical dimension. Every face is

"eclipsed by the lightening of the invisible"

as Adonis put it. It is a spiritual adventure. Like other great painters before him – Bonnard, Picasso, Rothko – Marwan has become ever bolder with age. From knots of colour, ephemeral dabs and lines in improvised, gesticulatory brushstrokes, he achieves a fullness that intensifies, in a series of visual metamorphoses, the closer we come to the painting; a glowing, trembling fullness that stands for a reconciliation of the self and the world, of the visible world and a different world.

What do I mean by this? Marwan is a painter, first and last. But he is also a mystic whose creative power is based equally in Western and Arab traditions, through which an inner beauty emerges in his paintings. It is a magic that is not static. In the stillness of his images we sense movement; in the emptiness of an eye we apprehend the universe. In this respect his paintings, by giving a reality to the invisible, are very near to poetry. The tracings of the hand endeavour to unlock the voice of the heart – and to join it to the sound of the world.

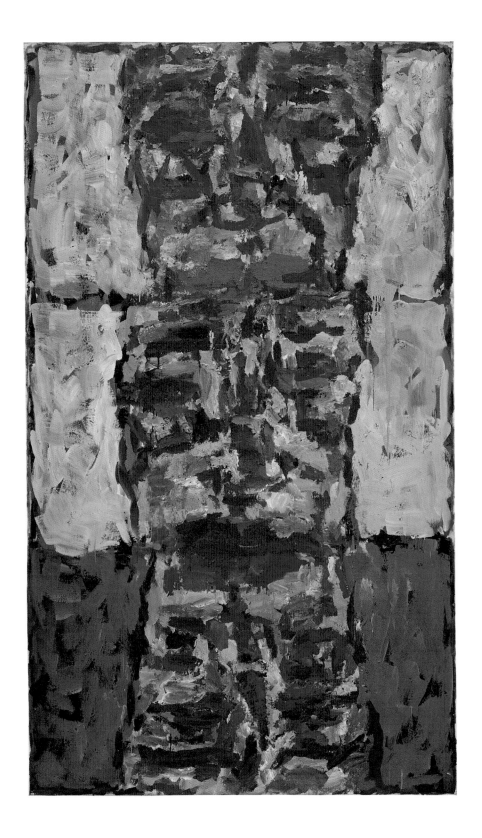

Robert Kudielka
Marwan paints a portrait

About two years ago Marwan told me that he would like to paint my portrait. My willingness may be taken as an example of how firm some of our strong convictions are grounded. As a rule I dislike pictures of me. Looking into the mirror in the early morning I often regret a certain deficiency in the male upbringing. Women probably would be as shocked by the sudden, always unexpected lack of recognition in that first encounter with one's appearance. It feels like waking up one day on a journey in a hotel room – and not knowing, for one perturbing moment, where you are. The only difference being that in this case the unknown place is your own face. But women either know or learn from early on that this is no revelation of truth, but a task to be tackled. You have to rigorously restore the self-recognition lost over night, to make yourself up for yourself and for the others, in order to preserve that stable, reliable mask without which no open exchange between people seems to be possible. Every morning I am impressed by those young girls sitting on the steps of my block of flats and smoking a last cigarette before they turn round the corner to submit to the ordeal of schooling. No matter what age or size they are, whether they are slim or plumb, they are almost indistinguishable for me, like a flock of birds, so well their faces are made up according to the latest girlie look.

However, the failure of unpremeditated recognition in the mirror is still rather harmless compared with the bewildering effect that photographs nearly always have on me. I simply can't understand people who hand around such souvenirs and, excitedly, point out to each other a certain spot, insisting: Look, there, in behind, the second one from the left – that's me! I encounter in such snap-shots most of the times two barely visible eyes, hidden behind half-shut lids, or a strangely gasping mouth, an exaggerated laughter showing too much teeth or the seemingly bad-tempered features of someone caught in absentia. Such lapses of composure are not completely alien to me. "Don't look so cross", friends sometimes admonish me when I' am sunk in thinking or try to listen to their arguments attentively. But catching and isolating these fugitive, involuntary poses leads to grotesque distortions: as though a madman got lost in a gallery of arrested life. This assessment is objective, confirmed by many witnesses. "Oh no, look at this", a press photographer to whom I was introduced as an important personality recently exclaimed, showing me on her digital camera her first score: "You don't look nearly as bad as that. Let's have a second shot!"

Portrait Azza Munif, 1999
Oil on canvas, 42 x 60 cm

Enough of this. Recounting some of my reservations only should underline that it was by no means vanity or the funny desire for being eternalised why I complied with Marwan's wish (which he, by the way, never explained) to paint a portrait. I really don't like any picture of me. Nevertheless, the prospect of visiting regularly, at least for a while, the studio in Schmargendorfer Straße and wasting time without pressure and remorse, unburdened by texts, projects and other imminent obligations, was very tempting. Marwan's old studio has been for me an oasis of civilisation in Berlin ever since we first met there in 1982. But apart from this personal motive there was yet another, more objective reason to set aside my apprehensions. Portraiture, which seems to be the most banal of all pictorial genres, is in fact one of the most mysterious. It shows its true artistic dimension at the very moment when its actual purpose has expired: when the person portrayed is either dead or forgotten and the resemblance no longer can be checked. The fame of such great portraitists as Holbein, Titian or Rembrandt rests upon the sheer incomparability of pictures that were commissioned and made with the intention to bear comparison with their living models. We are convinced that we somehow know the sitters – but whom do we recognise, given the fact that we barely know anything about their real presence? Paul Valéry tells the story of a friend who commented on

Portrait Laila Munif, 1999
Oil on canvas, 40 x 55 cm

the well-known portrait of Descartes by Frans Hals that the picture looked "very much alike". And indeed the slightly greasy locks framing the face and the steady look protruding from a pair of eyes set in deep sockets make this portrait of a Gitane-smoker avant le produit very suggestive … Yet Valéry is right in asking the poignant question: "ressemblant – à qui?" Resembling to whom?

So it was not only friendship, but also a certain curiosity whether in real life, as it were, one could perhaps find out more about this strange, seemingly unfounded similitude that in the summer of 2002 made me spent several hours as model in Schmargendorfer Straße. Every time I climbed up the stairs I enjoyed passing the other small enterprises in the building because for a writer even the names of workshops can have an enchanting effect. The appointment was usually in the afternoon, at Nietzsche's beloved hour, when the urgency of the day was easing off and the light started to soften, getting finer. The door often was open when I arrived. Marwan was busy with preparing Arabic coffee for his guest. As a kind of ritual we postponed the beginning of the work a little. I admired the view out of the big north window overlooking the roofs of the city, with a couple of handsome trees in the foreground (robinias, not acacias, he enlightened me). And then we took up our positions. I settled on a chair already placed in front of the west wall of the studio, where normally he worked his big paintings. At an oblique angle to the right I saw, in about three metres distance, the backside of the easel with the canvas on it; to my left, approximately half of this distance further removed, stood the painting table. In the open space between these two positions Marwan was moving.

Already during the first session I made a surprising discovery. In order to alleviate the tension and the burden of sitting I had begun to chatter in my most uninhibited, cheerful and wicked manner. Marwan is a fabulous listener, who can give one the feeling of conducting a conversation by responding with an understanding grin or a forgiving smile, or by interjecting a vigorous, encouraging "Aha". While this allowed him to fully concentrate on shifting his attention between painting table, canvas and my face, the horizon of my field of vision unwittingly was dropping – until I suddenly saw the unexpected: Marwan was wearing sports shoes, and by no means any odd gear, but the product of a well-known international brand. Of course anybody who is fashion-minded can put on such footwear. But that was not the point. It was the ease and assurance with which Marwan moved in this equipment, absolutely sportsmanlike, that was so astonishing.

It was not before the second meeting that I found the clue to this set up. The swift movements to and fro the canvas and the paint-

Studio Schmargendorfer Straße, 2002

ing table bore an unmistakable resemblance to the legendary "Ali Shuffle": floating like a butterfly and stinging like a bee. The parallel with the footwork of the great boxer was striking, disregarding his own, somewhat inaccurate metaphor. Butterflies do not dance - they flutter, drift or tumble in the air. But Marwan was dancing like The Champ himself: two or three bouncing steps forward, straight towards the painting; then a side-step, taking in the sight of the model and balancing the movements; after that the infight, the scrubbing, scratching noise of the brush on the canvas; and then back again, half-turned, almost on the heels, reverting to the painting table; there a kind of reassembling forces, cleaning the brush, changing colour, adding fresh pigment to the doe on the plate; eventually a short glance, checking the painting and the sitter; and then the renewed attack, two or three steps forward, etc. Thus we spent a good, generous, unlimited hour together, with a long, often speedy round at the beginning

Portrait Robert Kudielka, 2002
Oil on canvas

and a shorter, much slower one at the end. Each time we had a break in between, during which we had a cup of tea or coffee with cardamon and tried to conduct a relaxed conversation without stealing a premature glance at the state of the painting.

Nevertheless, as time went on the question of the final punch of the "Marwan Shuffle" became more and more pressing: Did he, this skilful dancer in the triangle of painting table, model and canvas, also perhaps "sting like a bee"? After the first meeting I was somewhat relieved to realise that the loose, patchy fabric on the canvas did not bear any resemblance, at least not for me, to anyone I knew. But this changed as the web of colours and brushmarks became denser and more coherent with every new layer, though not in the way of a cumulative clarification. Perfectly successful states of similitude disappeared as quickly and unexpectedly as they had emerged, in order to give way to new aspects and sometimes even a total breakdown of recognition. Meanwhile the tension grew. I am not sure whether it was in the second or in the third session that Marwan suddenly exchanged the small canvas, on which he had worked so far, for a bigger one, opening up a new, parallel approach. The art of picture-making had reached a critical stage Up until then he had worked almost exclusively on exploring the features of my head. But now he began to look for ways of locating and anchoring the image in the picture plane. Conversationally he mentioned that he had seen me wearing a dark blue vest – an apparently helpful detail. So next time I turned up in this piece of dressing in order to offer him a pretext to settle my head on shoulders. I also refrained from having my hair cut, hoping that this would prevent my skull from looking all too compact and isolated in space.

Unfortunately we didn't come to an end with this second painting. The last operation that I remember was rather drastic: with a broad brush Marwan coloured the surroundings of my head in thin, transparent washes of a slightly broken, brownish magenta – a typical "Marwan colour". This was the kind of punch that could have started a new round. But then the power of circumstances separated us. I had to enter hospital – and he had to leave his old, familiar studio. Only recently I have seen again the small first picture and I must admit that it looks very "alike", though in a completely modern sense. It cannot be judged under the traditional categories because it is neither a portrait exposing the character of an individual, nor is it a ritratto that truthfully renders the appearance of the sitter. There are of course features that I can recognise as belonging to me: the massive head, the asymmetrical, unfocused glance and the broad passage of the mouth. But the autonomous pictorial coherence of these characteristics does not allow for recognising an underlying identity: "It's me!" On the contrary, Marwan's art of portrayal reveals the very "veiled-ness" of one's identity, the many layers that in parts may obliterate one another and as a whole seem to constitute the opaque inner density of a person. In this way his portraits offer, as rare exceptions in his œuvre, an important hint on the understanding of his work in general.

I at least feel that this withdrawal of simple straightforward recognition provided "a good likeness of myself", as people say. Marwan made me resembling to me by withholding any conceivable image. Or if one last comparison with the boxing legend Muhammad Ali may be permitted: Marwan is neither a knock-outer nor an expert of tiny stings and stitches. His strategy is infinitely more refined. In dancing between the colour on the table, the canvas on the easel and my living presence, permanently shifting attention, he has step by step, both cautiously and cunningly, ensnared and captured myself, until eventually I looked on his canvas, unmistakably, like a genuine "Marwan".

Studio Schmargendorfer Straße, 2002

One-man shows

1967
– Galerie Springer, Berlin *

1969
– Privatgalerie Dr. Ammon, Berlin

1970
– Arabisches Kulturzentrum, Damascus *

1971
– Galerie Lietzow, Berlin *
– Galerie Medici, München

1972
– Galerie Lietzow, Berlin
– Privatgalerie Negendank, Trier
– Galerie Dr. Tscheuschner, Wuppertal

1973
– Einzelpräsentation der Galerie Lietzow auf der
  4. Internationalen Kunstmesse ART 4'73, Basel
– Galerie Pudelko, Bonn *

1974
– Privatgalerie Dr. Kaulen, Hannover
– Galerie Lietzow, Berlin

1975
– Galerie Buchholz, München *

1976
– Gruenebaum Gallery, New York *

– Galerie Lietzow, Berlin
– Orangerie Schloss Charlottenburg, Berlin *

1977
– Kunstschau-Böttcherstraße, Bremen
– Galerie Pudelko, Bonn
– Graphisches Kabinett Katrin Friebe, Darmstadt

1978
– Forum Kunst Rottweil
– Galerie Lietzow, Berlin

1980
– Museum of Modern Art, Bagdad *
– Galerie Lietzow, Berlin
– Galerie Marin, Hagen

1981
– Schloß Bellevue, Dokumenta-Archiv, Kassel *

1982
– Galerie Hartwig & Bethke, Berlin
– Galerie Dr. Tscheuschner, Kassel
– Galerie Timm Gierig, Frankfurt/Main

1983
– Overbeck-Gesellschaft Lübeck *
– Galerie Metta Linde, Lübeck
– Galerie Lietzow, Berlin
– Galerie Lietzow, Einzelpräsentation Kunstmarkt Köln

1984
– Kunsthalle Darmstadt *
– Galerie Joachim Becker, Cannes
– Galerie Bäumler, Regensburg

1985
– Galerie Wolfgang Ketterer, München *
– Studio-Galerie Hans Thoma-Gesellschaft, Reutlingen
– Galerie Lietzow, Berlin
– Einzelpräsentation Galerie Joachim Becker, Cannes,
  FIAC '85, XXIIème Foire International d'Art
  Contemporain de Paris, Grand-Palais

1986
– Galerie Timm Gierig, Frankfurt/Main
– Galerie Lüpfert, Hannover-Isernhagen
– Galerie Baumgarten, Freiburg
– Studio R., Mannheim

1987
– Galerie Springer, Berlin *
– Galerie Joachim Becker, Cannes
– Galerie Michael Hasenclever, München *
– Galerie Sfeir-Semler, Kiel *

1989
– Galerie Springer, Berlin *

1990
– Galerie Michael Hasenclever, München *
– Galerie Gardy Wiechern, Hamburg

– Galerie Metta Linde, Lübeck
– Galerie Joachim Becker, La Colle sur Loup / France

1991
– Galerie Tobias Hirschmann, Frankfurt/Main
– Kunststation St. Peter, Köln
– Haus der Kunst, München
– La Teinturerie Galerie, Paris
– Galerie Springer, Berlin *

1992
– Galerie Dube-Heynig, München
– Galerie Joachim Becker, Paris
– Busse Design, Ulm

1993
– Bibliothèque National de Paris *
– Institut du Monde Arabe, Paris *
– Galerie Tobias Hirschmann,Frankfurt/Main *
– Galerie Gaedy Wiechern, Hamburg
– Galerie Springer, Berlin
– La Teinturerie Galerie, Paris
– Galerie Joachim Becker, Paris

1994
– Galerie Atassi, Damaskus *
– Galerie d'Art 50 x 70, Beirut
– Galerie Tobias Hirschmann, Frankfurt/Main
– Galerie Dube-Heynig, München
– Galerie Springer, Berlin

1995
– Abdul Hameed Shoman Foundation,
  Darat al Funun, Amman *
– Galerie Atassi, Damaskus
– Galerie Studio R, Mannheim

1996
– Galerie Atassi, Damaskus, Retrospektive
– Al Hanager Hall, Kairo, Retrospektive
– Abdul Hameed Shoman Foundation,
  Darat al Funun, Amman, Retrospektive
1997
– Galerie Dube-Heynig, München

– La Teinturerie Galerie, Paris
– Volkan Galerie zeitgenössischer Kunst, Mainz

1998
– Birzeit University, Birzeit *
– Khalid Sakakini Cultural Centre, Ramallah *
– Abdul Hameed Shoman Foundation,
  Darat al Funun, Amman
– Raab Galerie, Berlin *
– Galerie épreuve d'artiste, Beirut

1999
– Galerie Hasenclever, München *
– Stadtmuseum Göhre, Jena *
– Galerie am Fischmarkt, Erfurt *
– Kunstverein Zweibrücken

2000
– Brechthaus Weissensee, Berlin

2001
– Khalil Sakakini Cultural Centre, Ramallah *
– Georg-Meistermann-Museum, Städtische Galerie
  für Moderne Kunst, Wittlich *
– Richard-Haizmann-Museum, Niebüll *

2002
– Galerie Dr. Irene Lehr, Berlin
– Lapidarium, Berlin
– Kunsthalle in Emden *

2003
– Galerie Linneborn, Berlin
– Vivantes, Berlin

2004
– Galerie Springer, Berlin
– Lippische Gesellschaft für Kunst, Detmold
– Khaled Shoman Foundation, Amman
– Charlier, Berlin

2005
– Art Convent de la misssió, Palma de Mallorca
– Damascus – Berlin – Damascus, Damascus *

– Solidere, Beirut *
– Lindenau-Museum in Altenburg, Altenburg *
– Ostdeutsche Landesbausparkasse Potsdam *

* catalogue

Work in public collections

Amman (Jordan)
— Abdul Hameed Shoman Foundation, Darat al Funun
— Arab Bank
— Khaled and Soha Shoman Collection

Berlin
— Staatliche Museen Preußischer Kulturbesitz: Nationalgalerie
  und Kupferstichkabinett
— Berlinische Galerie, Landesmuseum für Moderne Kunst,
  Photographie und Architektur
— Stiftung Archiv der Akademie der Künste
— Berliner Bank
— BerlinHyp

Birzeit (Palestine)
— Birzeit University

Bonn
— Kunstsammlungen der Bundesrepublik Deutschland

Bremen
— Kunsthalle Bremen

Coburg
— Graphische Sammlung der Veste Coburg

Damascus (Syria)
— Nationalmuseum Damaskus

Frankfurt/Main
— Deutsche Bundesbank

Göttingen
— Städtisches Museum Göttingen

Hamburg
— Hamburger Kunsthalle

Hannover
— Sprengel Museum Hannover

Jena
— Städtische Museen Jena, Romantikerhaus

Lübeck
— Museum für Kunst und Kulturgeschichte der Hansestadt
  Lübeck

Mannheim
— Städtische Kunsthalle Mannheim

Munich
— Bayerische Staatsgemäldesammlungen,
  Staatsgalerie moderner Kunst
— Staatliche Graphische Sammlung München

Oberhausen
— Ludwig Galerie Schloß Oberhausen

Oldenburg
— Landesmuseum Oldenburg

Paris
— Bibliothèque Nationale de France
— Institut du Monde Arabe

— Musée-Galerie de la Seita

Pittsburgh (USA)
— Carnegie Museum of Art

Potsdam
— Sammlung Ostdeutsche Landesbausparkasse LBS

Ramallah (Palestine)
— Khalil Sakakini Cultural Centre

Wolfsburg
— Städtische Galerie Wolfsburg

Head, 1976
Egg tempera, 195 x 130
Collection Kunsthalle Hamburg

Clayton Eshleman
Meditation on Marwan's faces
(1981)

The flats of the human face
will not admit (a mask). The ears,
jaws, cheeks (bent surfaces)
as they cry here mountainous colors
(worms), hurtled brows, worms of
mountains, husks of lean-to emotions,
arrogance dappled with
bringing arrogance closer,
gelid waterfalls of hares that do
not abstract out, but bronze, ruby snivels–

the flats, I repeat,
Marwan, whose peat rekneaded is
what Hades hides, our faces
the flat will not admit. The depth,
conceived on surface, is a depth I cannot
evade in mask. My leers, inabilities to walk
on a flat earth rounding me, reviling
Dachau months, they are available
because this man is not sure. Is not

surface, is not pure. Is
sink to the locust sensibility.
Eaten away, we are ripe, lame, the crux is
the human can be faced
but can the face be said in language?
Can a brittle alphabetic compost
zoom in on the hived
jungles cording Dis, the arachnoid trampoline,
the mast of bait coherent to another realm?

Head on, hand woven, a mandala of
tufts and thread taken apart, the human face
is a twisting warren, wave on wave of
tunneled crimson, days of napalm, nights
of azure peace. It is a kind of rug
before its shape is fixed-in Marwan's
works-in a between that is not
a mystical point between us
but a depth between the deathmask of the Covering
Persona and peeled off skin.

In this depth both mask and meat are included
in the impasto of pus-like fibers,
a rabbit flayed in romantic gondola,
moments of unchanging plaster, streaked
by weeping caked with first fruits,
the cenote of the eye
limpid, greased by the plunging
flecks of things as they sacrifice
into our hollows, and our faces fill,
empty with passing through
and over, under Narcissus–

is it that echo died and then
a youth fell to adore the labyrinth in water,
or is that the import of what
we see becomes an echo
at the moment we reflect, and reflecting
weave on surface, milling this crisis
into mental walls, in the twist of which
we anticipate a face, more coarse more
animal than ours, a furred muzzle that in dream

begins to reassemble on our chests
animal grief entombed in nightmare,
pounding on our heart *Let me in.*
Not the fantasy of a childhood locked out,
crying for its parents … No, let me fold
that in, call it a minor green
but because it occurs allow it as part
of the supreme lock-out.

Dream muzzle wants in to a place we
no longer are, or only are in imagination,
a place so remote it is hardly hard of our becoming–
more, it is the being
at the heart of becoming, the unchanging
kernel in the loosening hull of the human face,
chamber of the anthrobeast,
visible in these Marwan eyes, vaulted at the brow,
steeply recessing vaginal folds of stone
darken to the chink through which we enter Niaux

Head, 1994
Oil on canvas, 162 x 260

The Friend, 2000 / 01
Oil on canvas, 195 x 260 cm

Reflection, 2000
Oil on canvas, 146 x 97 cm

Head, 1995
Oil on canvas, 97 x 130 cm

Head, 1996
Oil on canvas, 130 x 195 cm

The Friend, 2001 / 02
Oil on canvas, 229 x 325 cm

The Friend, 2004
Oil on canvas, 162 x 228 cm

The Friend, 2001 / 02
Oil on canvas, 146 x 228 cm

The Friend, 2000 / 01
Oil on canvas, 114 x 162 cm

Head, 2004
Oil on canvas, 162 x 130 cm

Head, 1995
Oil on canvas, 130 x 97 cm

Opposite:
Head, 2004
Oil on canvas, 228 x 162 cm

The Friend, 2002
Oil on canvas, 130 x 140 cm

Head, 1996
Oil on canvas, 162 x 195 cm

Head, 1995 / 96
Oil on canvas, 114x 146 cm

Head, 1999
Oil on canvas,
162 x 130 cm

Opposite:
Head, 1998
Oil on canvas,
146 x 97 cm

Opposite:
Reflection, 2002
Oil on canvas, 195 x 114 cm

Head, 2003
Oil on canvas, 130 x 162 cm

Preceding page left:
Head, 1992
Oil on canvas, 146 x 114 cm

Preceding page right:
Head, 2003
Oil on canvas, 146 x 114 cm

مروان

مروان

دمشق – برلين – دمشق

خان أسعد باشا

دمشق، نيسان ٢٠٠٥

صدر هذا الكاتلوج بمناسبة معرض

«مروان»

دمشق ـ برلين ـ دمشق

فكرة وإشراف: منى أتاسي
تنظيم: معهد غوتيه دمشق، مانفرد إيڤل
سينوغرافيا: حكمت شطَا
تصميم وإخراج: يزن قصَاب باشي، برلين
تنضيد: حسن الشامي، برلين
تصوير الأعمال: يورغ ب. أندرس، يوخن ليتكامن،
      رومان مارتس، مروان
تصوير توثيقي: يزن قصاب باشي، يورن ماركرت،
      محمد الرومي، غيرت ميلتينغ،
      آنيا مورينغ، يونس فون شفيدس
فرز وطباعة: روكسال دروك، برلين

شكر خاص:
وزارة الثقافة، الوزير الدكتور محمود السيد
وزارة المغتربين، الوزيرة الدكتورة بثينة شعبان
السفارة السورية في برلين، السفير الدكتور حسين عمران
سوليدير، السيد ناصر الشمَاع، بيروت

برعاية بعثة الوحدة الأوروبية ـ سوريا

مروان ودمشق

بعد نحو خمسين عاماً من العيش والعمل في برلين، وبعد تحقيق إبداع متميز، ما زال الرسام السوري المولد بحاجة إلى أن يكتشف من قبل ناسه في موطنه. لقد عرضت لوحاته في كثير من المتاحف والصالات في جميع أنحاء أوروبا، وفي مصر والأردن وفلسطين. إلا أن ما ينقص حتى الآن هو معرض لائق للوحاته في سوريا ولبنان. وبفضل جهود صالة الأتاسي تحققت إمكانية مشاهدة بعض أعماله في دمشق عام ١٩٩٦. ولكن الآن فقط سيتاح لجمهور مدينته أن يتملى في أهم لوحاته في أحد أشهر الأمكنة التاريخية في المدينة.

بالتعاون مع صالة الأتاسي ووزارة الثقافة السورية يتشرف معهد غوته بتقديم مروان في كثير من سماته الفنية والإنسانية: فحتى من موطنه في برلين كان مروان على صلة وثيقة بروائيين وشعراء عرب متميزين. إن عمله كرسام ومصور إلى جانب تدريسه لسنوات طويلة في أكاديمية الفنون البرلينية قد استفاد دائماً من حساسيته لذكر يات وألوان وشعرية الأصوات في مسقط رأسه.

وهذا هو السبب الذي جعلنا لا نكتفي بعرض بعض أهم أعماله من مراحل مختلفة فحسب، بل دفعنا إلى أن ندعو مجموعة من رفاق حياة مروان لتكريم منجزاته كفنان وإنسان مبدع. فسواء في لوحاته أو في تدريسه شجع مروان كثيراً من ذوي الحساسية المرهفة على اكتشاف جوهر الفن البصري، وإمكانية فهمه، على الرغم من المسافات الجغرافية والخلفيات الثقافية المختلفة.

وأخيراً يود منظمو هذا الحدث أن يعبروا عن شكرهم إلى الاتحاد الأوروبي وإلى كافة الممولين الآخرين لدعمهم الثمين في تقديم هذا الحدث إلى الفنانين والمهتمين بالفن في دمشق.

مانفرد إيفل

مدير معهد غوته – دمشق

هل ثمّة كلام لم يُقال بعد في مروان ؟ لا أظنّ.

فهذا الرجل الذي أعرفه لا يواسيه بعد اليوم كلام، بل مكان ضيّع ساعة الرحيل عنوانه.

مكان حمل منه مروان صرّة أحلام، وعدّة رسم، وشتلة حنين، ومفتاح دار، ميمّماً شطر الشمال.

هناك، مزمز أحلامه، حلماً بعد حلم، قرابة نصف قرن، بأنانية الطفل الذي يأبى الفطام،

وهناك، فرد عدّته، وأفرغ أصباغه، وأعمل فراشيه، فنال المجد واستحق الثناء،

وهناك، في صقيع الليل الرماديّ الطويل، وتحت وسادة «أناه» المنشغلة بذاتها، نمت شتلة حنين وذبل الشوق،

وهناك أخيراً، حيث لا خلود لغربة، ولا مفتاح لجنّة، ولا عبق لآس، لملم مروان من بستان إبداعه، وأقحوان فنّه، باقة من عمرٍ للتي لم تنساه يوماً، ولم يفارقها لحظة: دمشق.

منى أتاسي

غاليري أتاسي

٥

يورْن ميرْكيرْت

غريبٌ في العالم أو صورٌ للظمآن
عن مروان

«الغريب، هو الغريب في الغربة فقط»

كارل فلانتين

سحر

لطالما سحرني عالم لوحات مروان طوال الخمس وعشرين سنة الماضية. كان
يبدو لي دائماً غريباً ومألوفاً في آن معاً. وتماماً بمعنى حلم اليقظة الطوباوية
الملموسة عند إرنست بلوخ، يحمل هذا العالم في داخله غربة آتية من مكان
قصي ومليئة بالوعود. وهذا السحرُ يمتلك المشاهد بشكل مباشر وغير مباشر.
فعلى الرغم من أن فن مروان مغلف في إهاب ثمين من الرسم الأوربي، إلا أن
هذا الإهاب لا يغطي ملامح غير مرئية بعد بشكل كامل. إن عالمه مشحون
بموسيقية خاصة جداً ومترع بتلوين حسي جريء بإيقاعات نادرة. كما يفوح
منه عبق لا ينتمي إلى هذا العالم الغربي. كل ما فيه يولّد شعوراً بالحنين،
بـ«ملنقولية» هادئة فرحة، بألم عميق، وبقلب جذِل – من دون أي انجراف
أدبي، بل بالتجلي المرئي فحسب، باللون والشكل، حسياً وروحياً. وهكذا يتلقى
المشاهد غير الخبير بوساطة أحاسيسه الذاتية انطباعات عفوية أولية، سرعان
ما تطرح الأسئلة حول: من أين، وإلى أين، ولماذا؟ ولكن أن يشير الإنسان
ببساطة إلى أصل الفنان القادم من أطراف الصحراء والواحات وحدائق
وأسواق دمشق المشمسة، فهذا يعني فك السحر عن السر الثمين بسعر بخس .

لذلك لن ننشغل الآن بسيرة نشأته، بل لاحقاً. أما الآن فهي ليست أكثر من مفتاح
إلى مدخل السر الذي ينطوي عليه فن مروان. إن من ينساق وراء لوحات مروان
من دون تحفظات، فإنها ستورطه في حوار حميمياً عفوياً ومفاجئاً.
وقد يكون الأمر صادماً، لأننا لسنا دائماً على استعداد لذلك، على صعيد
التعامل مع الفن؛ أو قد يكون على الأقل مفاجئاً، لأننا نجد أنفسنا أمام هذه
اللوحات ومن دون أي تحفظ – لا إرادياً وبلا وعي – نخوض حواراً أحادياً مع

الزقاق، ١٩٥٦.

زيت على ورق، على خشب، ٢٧ × ٢٣ سم.

وعن أنفسنا. بداية، ومن دون أية معرفة مسبقة، تروي لنا هذه الغربة الخاصة والمؤثرة في لوحات مروان عن الخسارة والقصور، عن قصور المُشاهد أيضاً. إذ إن الحنين الذي توحي به لوحاته، ليس فقط حنين الفنان الشخصي، بل هو كامن في كل منا، وهذا ما يجعله ينهض من الذاكرة محسوساً. إلا أنه من الطبيعي أن الأمل الذي يستدعي إلى الذاكرة الأفضل والمغاير لكل فرد منا، يرتبط لدى كل منا بمكان آخر، قد يكون واحة فردية لذاك الذي يشعر هناك بالعطش. إن الفن دائماً ذو بُعدٍ طوباوي، أي أنه صادق، وهو هنا يذكرنا بجوعنا جميعاً إلى أمور مضت، وأخرى سيحملها إلينا المستقبل، كما يجعلنا ندرك في الوقت نفسه أن الحاضر لم يتحقق كلياً بعد. إن الفن يذكرنا دائماً بالفردوس المفقود، لكنه يحفظه أيضاً ككنز ثمين، كوعد يتحول في أثناء رحلة الحياة إلى التزام.

إن ما يبقى مثيراً للدهشة – وهو ما يمنحنا أول مؤشر موثوق عبر هذا العالم الغريب – هو أن هذا الإنسان خلال تجواله، قد تطور كثيراً على ما يبدو، خلال خمسين سنة من الممارسة الفنية، لكنه بقي رغم ذلك هو نفسه كلياً ودائماً. وحتى عندما بدا أنه يسير على الطريق الخاطئة، فتاه عبر صحارى نادرة الواحات؛ حتى عندها، كان يتجلى رسمٌ ما، غير واضح المعالم من حيث صلته بالحاضر، حسبما بدا له، ولكن بالعودة في الذاكرة، سرعان ما يتبدى الرسم جزءاً من كلٍ، في نظام يفتح للمعنى أفقاً أرحب وأعمق. الأمر الذي يخلق عند اليأس ثقة بالنفس، من دون أن يُخمد القلق المندفع، بل يوقظه باتجاه جديد. ولكأن مروان كان منذ البداية على علم بجملة بلوخ التي تبدو بسيطة: «أنا كائن. لكنني لا أملك نفسي. ولهذا فإننا نصير».[1] إلّا أن هذا تأويل أوروبي، لا يولي الغربة ما يكفي من الاهتمام.

ومع ذلك يتجلى في ما يرسمه مروان – وطبعاً وبالتحديد في كيفية رسمه – إلى أي مدى، وكم هو مروان دائماً عند نفسه. عند هذه الأنا كائن. «يتجلى مدى جوعه وعطشه، وكيف ينطلق من جديد دائماً وراء البحث الذي لا ينتهي، عن هذه الـ أنني لا أملك نفسي.» وكيف أدرك مبكراً أن الهدف ليس ثابتاً، وأنه لا يرتبط بمكان واحد مرة وإلى الأبد، بل أن الإنسان يحمل وطنه الحي معه في

١– إرنست بلوخ - Ernst Bloch مدخل إلى الفلسفة في توبينغن، الجزء الأول، فرانكفورت ١٩٦٨، ص١١.

طبيعة صامتة، ١٩٨٣.

زيت على قماش، ٨٩ x ١١٦ سم.

ذاته، وهو الوطن الذي قد يصل إليه ربما ثانية، بنموه داخلياً بصورة شاملة، وهو الوعد الذي يمنح الفنان الأملَ ويُلزمه في آن معاً: فلهذا فإننا «نصير». ليس لوحدنا، إنما في الحوار مع «أنتَ العالم» حسب تعبير باول كليه. أو بالوعي الدقيق بأننا، في حتمية قدرنا بين الولادة والموت، جزء لا يتجزأ من الخلق وفي الخلق.

إن ما يرسمه مروان هو صور بشر، التقطت من آنية اللحظة، مراراً وتكراراً، نبع لا ينضب من صور بشر، يتجلى فيها كل شيء مرئياً، وتسائل كل شيء، وتقول ما لا يمكن أن يقال، وتجعل ما لم يشاهَد سابقاً مدرَكاً. وهناك بعض لوحات الطبيعة الصامتة، إلاّ أنها قليلة نسبياً. وهي متخمة بالشعور بالامتلاك الحسي، بحيث تجعل ما يبدو صامتاً في الظاهر، يتجلى مترعاً بحيوية العالم. وهكذا تستطيع الدمية أيضاً، الشيء الذي لا حياة فيه، الموهوب بالمشاعر في الفن، أن تصير صورة بشر. إن هذا الطرف النقيض للأنا – ومرة ثانية «أنت العالم» – يصبح بالمقدار نفسه مغوياً، معزّياً، مستفزاً، مغناجاً، لعوباً، ممتلئاً بالشوق، ممانعاً ومعانقاً، معطاءً ومفكراً مصغياً إلى داخله – وخائفاً أيضاً لكنه ممتلئ بالمرح – كذات الأنا عندما تلتفت إلى الأنت.

في وقت مبكر من شبابه في دمشق وحولها، رسم مروان قليلاً من المناظر الطبيعية – وفي بعض هذا القليل تظهر شخوص منعزلة. لكنه لن يحتاج إليها في ما بعد. لا لأنه يحمل هذه الصور في ذاته فحسب، ولا لأن الطبيعة كانت عزيزة عليه جداً في شبابه – وهي كذلك في الشرق عامة – بحيث لا يجرؤ على تحريك هذه الذكرى. لا، وإنما لأنه لم يعد بحاجة إلى رسم مناظر طبيعية، منذ أن تمكن من جعل كل الخبرة الحسية المرتبطة بالطبيعة المحيطة تتسرب بكل بداهة إلى صور البشر التي يرسمها – وليس فقط إلى لوحاته الموسومة بـ «وجوه مشهديّة».

إن عالم مروان الفني يتشكل من البشر ومن طبيعة الأشياء الصامتة ومن المناظر الطبيعية الداخلية. ومن هذه الموضوعات القليلة والقريبة والبسيطة جداً يشيّد مروان كونه الفني. هذا هو كل شيء، وهو يبدو شحيحاً، لكنه في الحقيقة يشمل كل شيء، من التنوع الذي لا ينضب كالطبيعة، ومن المدى اللامحدود والكثافة الضاغطة كالمناظر الطبيعية المسكونة بلحظة الأبدية – خاصة وفي المقام الأول عندما تكثفت موضوعاته الثلاثة الكبرى خلال العقدين الأخيرين إلى صور «رؤوس» فحسب، إلى مناظر أرواح وجودنا.

لقد بقي مروان حتى اليوم غريباً في العالم. وفي الحقيقة لا لأنه فقط قد هاجر من الشرق إلى الغرب، حيث بنى عالمه هنا. فالغربة سرنا جميعاً، وعن طريقها نفهم الحياة. أما بالنسبة إلى مروان، فالغربة ليست شرطاً وجودياً فحسب، بل هي بالدرجة نفسها بؤرة الحنين. فمن البعيد يتراءى لنا المألوف جداً، غريباً بصورة مؤلمة عذبة. إن مروان يعيش هذه الغربة ويخبرنا عنها في

خيمة بلّورة، ١٩٥٤،
زيت على قماش، ٣٠ x ٣٩ سم.

جميع لوحاته. إن حالة الشعور بالغربة هي البوابة المشرعة على كل شيء، فهي دائماً تجربة حدودية. وتجاوز الغريب يعني خلق الفرح، أي التعرية والبحث عن الحقيقة. لكن الإنسان لا يستطيع دائماً أن يكون قريباً. أما الابتعاد المجدَّد فيعيد خلق الغربة، حتى وإن كان الإنسان الآن أكثر معرفة: عندها يصير النأي حجاباً يخفي سراً نعرفه، ويوقظ الحنين. وحركة المشاعر المتأرجحة كالنواس بين القرب والنأي، بين الأمل والتحقق، بين الخسارة المؤلمة والذكرى المبهجة، بين البحث والعثور؛ إن مكوك النسّاج هذا، الذي لا يغني عن الحركة المتكررة ذهاباً وإياباً في حياة البشر، بين الروح والقلب، هو ما ترجمته لوحات مروان بشكل ساحر وفي تجلٍّ مرئي مباشر.

وجه مشهدي، ١٩٧٢.

تمبرا البيض على قماش، ١٩٥ x ٢٦٠ سم.

مجموعة المتحف الوطني للفن الحديث، برلين

لقاء

عرفت مروان قبل أن نلتقي. لا بد أن الأمر يعود إلى عام ١٩٧٠، عندما كان مدير المتحف الوطني فرنر هافتمن (Werner Haftmann)، يعلق لوحتين مائيتين غريبتين: الوجوه فيهما ممطوطة طولانياً كما في المرايا المقعرة، والألوان بنية في بنية، مع شيء من اللون الأمغر، وربما الأصفر، أما الألوان الأخرى فلم أرغب حتى في رؤيتها. لقد منعت نفسي بكل بساطة عن أن أتأثر بها، والأصح: لم أرد بأي حال من الأحوال أن يؤثر فيّ ما أراه. كنت ممتلئاً بالأحكام المسبقة الشبابية، غارقاً في الفن المعاصر؛ ولما كانت عيناي ورأسي متخمة من البوب آرت والهابينينغ والفلوكْسَس، فقد شعرت بأن أعمال هذا السوري في برلين في غاية الغرابة، وبأنها في المكان غير المناسب والتوقيت الخاطئ. أي أنها في نظري خارج الموضة كلياً. ولم يستطع حتى معلمي هافتمن الذي أكنّ له كل الاحترام، أن يفتح عيني على كون هذه الأعمال بتقنياتها الموروثة حالة مغايرة تماماً لكل ما هو تقليدي. وبعد فترة من الزمن أضيفت على اللوحتين المائيتين لوحة جديدة، وكانت «وجه مشهدي» من عام ١٩٧٢. بقيت أعمى، وانسحبت، لم أتدخل وأغلقت نفسي تجاه ما كان قد أثّر فيّ حتماً، وإلاّ لما حملت عنه في نفسي مثل هذه الذكريات الحية. لكنني لم أسائل نفسي عن التجربة الخاصة، التي رفضتها عفوياً ولا إرادياً، ولكأنها تشكل خطرا مهدداً، أو أن شخصاً غير مرغوب فيه قد اقترب مني أكثر مما يجب.

وقد لاحظت الأمر نفسه لدى آخرين، وما زال الأمر على ما هو عليه حتى اليوم: فمن يرى لوحات مروان لأول مرة، سرعان ما يغلق نفسه في وجهها غالباً، كردّ فعل دفاعي، أو يسقط أسير غوايتها. إذ يستحيل أن يبقى المرء حيالها فاتراً من دون مشاركة. أما من ينفتح حيالها حقيقة، فإنها تتغلغل إلى روحه.

إن الأحكام المسبقة، ولا سيما إن كانت غير مسلحة إلاّ بالغرور الشبابي وقلة الخبرة النسبية، قد تكون عنيدة جداً وغير قابلة للاختراق، لأنها لا تخفي شك القلق وعدم اليقين والجهل. وفي عام ١٩٧٥ عندما كنت في الثامنة والعشرين من عمري قمت بزيارة مروان، مزوداً بشكوكي وبأحكامي المسبقة في جعبتي٢. وكان ذلك في مرسمه في شارع شمارغنْ دورْف. ولكن عندما غادرته بعد ساعات لم أعد أعرف عددها، وقد مرت وكأنها لحظة فحسب، كنت في حقيقة الأمر مسحوراً. علماً بأن المرسم في حد ذاته لم يكن مثيراً أو لافتاً. أما مروان فقد استقبلني بودّ وقدم لي الشاي. وحتى اليوم ما زال أول ما يقدمه مروان هو الشاي، دائماً. ثم أراني في المرسم الواسع الذي ما زال فارغا، عدداً من اللوحات. وبالإعتماد على ذاكرتي، كان الحوار في البداية شحاً متردداً، لكن مشاهدة اللوحات كانت فترات صمت مشحونة بالكثير من الكلام. لم يُرني اللوحات بالطريقة التي اعتدتها، لوحة بعد أخرى، بأن يسند اللوحة على

الجدار أو يعلقها عليه. لا، بل كان يوزعها بعناية في فضاء المرسم – وهذه طريقته حتى اليوم في عرض الصور للمشاهدة – بحيث تستند اللوحة إلى نقطة واحدة، ككرسي أو طاولة، ثم تتبعها اللوحة الثانية ملامسة إياها بلطف، وهكذا تصطف شيئاً فشيئاً بانوراما كاملـة من اللوحات في توازن بالغ الهشاشة عبر فضاء المرسم كله. وإذا امتدت اللوحات على امتداد المكان، وإذا لم يشبع الإنسان من المشاهدة، عندها يأتي صف ثان أو ثالث من اللوحات. وفي النهاية وقفت بين اللوحات كمن يقف في حديقة وسط امتدادات أزهارها وورودها الرائعة. كنت في غاية الهدوء وشعرت بنفسي أتذكر قول هاينريش فون كلايست: Heinrich von Kleist «وكأن جفني عيني قد بُترا.»

إن تأثير عرض اللوحات بهذا الأسلوب غير المستقر، يولّد الإحساس بها كشيء ثمين بشكل خاص، لأنها تتبدى للرؤية فعلاً. فتتراءى ولو للحظة واحدة. لا يمكن أن تقف اللوحاتُ طويلاً على هذا الشكل (يقول في نفسه زائر المرسم غير الخبير)، إذ هناك خطر دائم بأن تهوي بسرعة فتصاب بالأذى. آنذاك، لم أدرك للتو، لكنني عايشت بعمق شديد كيف أن هذا الأسلوب في العرض ينسجم تماماً مع مضمون وشكل وشخصية عالم لوحات مروان. فاللوحات في ذاتها تكون غالباً وبالفعل ظاهرة؛ فهي في خطاطتها السريعة لتكويناتها الحركية، وفي خط ريشتها المتأني والخاطف بالدرجة نفسها، توحي بأنها عابرة وفي غاية الرقة؛ وهذه الرقة التي تنطوي عليها اللوحات تظهر في التعامل الملموس معها، وبهذا الأسلوب يوضع المشاهد في الجو الملائم لتلقيها. إنها تحمل ما هو زمني وعابر: فيحتاج المشاهد لمدة من الوقت كي يستعد لقراءتها، ولكن ما إن يصل إلى لحظة المعرفة الإدراكية حتى تنسحب منه اللوحات ثانية إلى بقايا آثار رسم، غير مترابطة ومتحللة ومنفتحة كلياً. وغالباً ما يؤدّي القرب الكبير، بل الضاغط لتجسيد الوجوه والشخوص بهذا الأسلوب الإخراجي للوحات إلى تصعيد التأثير.

إن زائر المرسم يتعرض في أثناء زياراته بشكل إيحائي تماماً إلى نوع من المشاهدة المكوكية والدائرية رغم التركيز كله، إلى مشاهدة عابرة لا واعية؛ تماماً كما في هذه اللوحات الصامتة التي تكاد أن تنسكب منها أحياناً تخمة حقيقية من أفعال الرسم، هكذا تتجول النظرة من قماشة مرسومة إلى أخرى، مستوعبة إياهـا وكل شيء في اللحظة نفسها، مع الرغبة في امتصاصها للذات، بغية إشباع النظرة وإطفاء عطش العينين للون.

مرسم شمارغن دورف، سنة ٢٠٠٢.

٣- مقبوس عن: يوهانَس أودنتال Johannes
Odenthal – سوريا – حضارة راقية بين البحر
الأبيض المتوسط والصحراء العربية، دو مونت
دليل رحلات فني، كولونيا، ١٩٩٥، ص ٧٠.

في عام ١٩٧٣ عاش مروان سنة كاملة في باريس، بمنحة من مؤسسة «مدينة الفنون» حيث تعرض أسلوبه إلى انعطافة جزئية بفعل الانطباع الداهم لكل من سيزان، مونيه، مانيه، كوربيه وسوتين. لم أعرف آنئذ أن عام ١٩٧٣ قد حقق له حلماً من أحلام شبابه، وبصورة ناجحة... ولكن لننتهز الفرصة كي نستعيد درجات تحولات فن مروان باسترجاعات منتظمة، وهي مغامرة عقل وحس في حياة رسام.

إنطلاق مبكر

في كتابه الضخم عن سيرة مروان العربية، يترك عبد الرحمن منيف الفنان يتحدث عن طفولته ويفاعته في دمشق بتفهم عميق ملح، بحيث تفهم حتى الآذان الأوربية، أن هذا العالم قد ضاع إلى الأبد. كما يتحدث منيف، عن ذاته أيضاً، بأسلوب يبدو لنا، حتى في بداهته وعاديته، كحكاية خرافية عجيبة، تحمل في نسماتها خدْر عبق الزهور والفواكه والبهارات، وثمة ضوء ساطع يجعل كل شيء يتلألأ: ألوان الحدائق النضرة والعباءات والأسواق، وقد غشتها أصوات هادئة متسربة من حياة غابرة؛ صوت سائق عربة هنا، وصرير دواليب طنبر هناك، خرير مياه النافورة من هنا، وغناء عندليب من هناك، ووقع شديد لحوافر خيول على حجارة الطريق، يخفت تحت الأشجار وتبتلعه رمال الصحراء – إنه عالم مروان. إلاّ أنه لم يختف فحسب، مثلما تتحول كل طفولة إلى حلم. فالخسارة أكبر من ذلك، أكبر بكثير؛ فالعالم الذي يحكي لنا منيف عنه قد تهاوى في اضطرابات الشرق الأوسط السياسية التي كادت أن تسحق سوريا القديمة بين وطأة التاريخ والحداثة المدمّرة. وعلى الرغم من ذلك ما زال وعي الناس يحتفظ بالحلم العتيق الحقيقي عن المدينة المقدسة ومنذ أزمان غابرة: «والله، لقد صدق الذين قالوا: إن كان ثمة جنة على الأرض فهي دمشق، وإن كانت الجنة في السماء، فدمشق هي مقابلها الأرضي»٣. كما ورد على لسان الرحالة الأندلسي ابن جبير في الخامس من تموز عام ١١٨٤ عن هذه البوتقة التي يعود عمرها إلى عشرة آلاف سنة، والتي انصهرت فيها الشعوب ولغاتها ودياناتها.

لقد تمكن مروان من الحفاظ على عدد لا بأس به من اللوحات التي رسمها في شبابه. وهي بورتريهات ومناظر طبيعية. وعلى حيرته الأسلوبية المفهومة تبدو هذه اللوحات في العين الغربية تعبيراً عن ثقة مدهشة بالنفس، وعن الطزاجة والجو الذي خلقته حركات فرشاته اللينة والممتدة. ولكأن مروان منذئذ قد شاهد لوحات انطباعية، أو سيزان في لوحاته غير المكتملة، أو الالتماع الشفيف في بعض لوحات بونار أو فويار. قد يكون رآها في كتب غربية أو في مجلات فنية أجنبية، ولكن ليس في نسخ عن الأصل، وإن كان هذا قد حدث، فبألوان رديئة. ولكن كم كان الأمر بسيطاً بالنسبة لهذا الشاب أن

يرى ألوان عالمه في النُسَخ، أو أن يحلم بها هناك – فتوقظ في نفسه التوق لأن يراها في بهاء الأصل، ذات يوم، أو لأن يرسم بنفسه مثل هذه الروعة.

إن لوحات المناظر الطبيعية المبكرة التي تمس عيوننا مساً تبدو للوهلة الأولى بريئة تماماً، إلا أنها في الواقع ليست كذلك. إن بذرة الشوق إلى أوربا، إلى هذا العالم الغريب، كانت قد زرعت بهذه اللوحات. وكان اسم الحلم باريس.

يبدو أن الشك لم يراوده مطلقاً في أنه سيصير رساماً، في أنه يريد هذه المهنة. ومن المدهش أن نرى كيف حضّر مروان نفسه فكرياً بصورة جيدة، لانطلاقه في الرحلة نحو الغرب. فبشكل مفاجئ سرعان ما اتخذ رسمه تجسيداً مغايراً تماماً – وجلي للعيان أن ذلك كان بتأثير لوحات أوربية من القرن العشرين. لكنه ما كان قادراً على رؤيتها في أصولها. فإذا كان فضاء المنظر الطبيعي المنعكس بأمانة من حيث جوه، هو موضوعه المنفذ بضربات ريشة مقتصدة في توزيع اللون، فقد أصبح سطح اللوحة فجأة انعكاساً تاماً لما هو عليه في الواقع: مسطحاً. أصبحت هندسة اللوحة تتشكل من حقول لون ممتدة وقليلة، متراصفة أو متقاطعة. إن النظام اللوني الواضح والمحافظ على بساطته التامة في لوحات ماتيس يتبدى أمامنا عن بعد بشكل لا تخطئ العين تأثيره المباشر.

ولكن في لوحة مثل «الإبريق» من عام ١٩٥٦ عندما كان مروان في الثانية والعشرين من عمره، نجده في لغة اللوحة الغربية قد استعاد بشكل جلي عالمه الشرق أوسطي. اللونان البني والأمغري هنا – طبيعويان تقريباً من حيث الاستخدام المادي – هما طبعاً تكثيف لوني للصحراء والحجر والأرض الخصبة؛ والألوان تغطي مساحة اللوحة كلها بحركات دائرية كالأخاديد، ولم يعد هناك فضاء مجسد، بل كل شيء صار مسطحاً – كما لو جلس أحدهم متربعاً ومرر يده عبر الأرض الرملية.

بهذا المنظور القريب والذي لا يمتلك أفقاً، دخل إلى اللوحة في الوقت نفسه المدى اللامحدود للمنظر وبشكل مبهر. والذي يعيش هناك لا يحتاج إلا للقليل، لما لا يمكن الاستغناء عنه: للجرة الفخارية ذات القبضة الواسعة الموشاة بما يشبه الأرابسك والميزاب الذي يمثل تدفق نهر الماء الثمين، ثم هناك الليمونة، مثال الإنعاش، وهي ثمرة لذيذة اسْتُنبتت بعون الله والعمل المجهد من التربة الفقيرة. كما أن هناك العين، عين فاطمة التي تدفع الشر بعيداً. فالله قريب في كل شيء.

في الثالثة والعشرين رسم مروان لوحة (المستحمة) ستُعد استباقاً للآتي: منظر خلفي لفتاة تلبس بجسد أصفر، ورأسها محاط بشعر أسود يُنصّفه مفرق طولاني حاد، ويتدلى من ثم في ضفيرة طويلة تقسم الجسد الأصفر إلى قسمين. وهي تجلس على حجر أسود في ليلة حالكة متلألئة بالنجوم. هذا هو كل شي. صورة حلم. صورة حنين طفلة حالمة تحت خيمة مرصعة بالنجوم. وقد

مأذنة القاسمية، ١٩٥٤.

زيت على قماش، ٣٠ X ٣٩ سم.

المستحمة، ١٩٥٧.

زيت على قماش، ٤٨٫٥ X ٣٦ سم.

تحولت حرارة النهار غير المتراجعة إلى ضياء مبهر في ثوبها، بينما يرخي الليل برودته. كل شيء مغلف بالسر، فالصورة لا تكشف عن أي شيء. الفتاة تجلس ملتفتة عنا، غارقة في نفسها – ونحن مشاهدون نسبغ على المشهد أحلامنا الخاصة. وها نحن ثانية نرى هندسة الرسم اللونية الصارمة والحرة تماماً والمسطحة، كما نعرفها عن ماتيس، ولكن ثانية أيضاً نجد كل شيء حقيقياً مشرّباً بأحاسيس آتية من البعيد، من العالم العربي الغريب عنا – حتى وإن لم نستطع أن نفسر كيف نجح مروان في ذلك. كيف كان للأمر أن يجري على نحو آخر، فيفكر الأوربي طبعاً بـ كاسبار دافيد فريدريش Caspar David Friedrich وبالشخوص البارزة الألوان في لوحاته التي تجذب الرؤية إلى داخل الفضاء المرسوم. ولكن حين يكون الحنين ملتصقاً بالموضوع، في التفكير الأوربي لدى كاسبار دافيد فريدريش – برمز السفينة مثلاً – يكون لدى مروان سواد السماء، بهذا التجريد والاتصال الروحي عن طريق الكلمة بالكون.

يختلف الأمر في لوحة «صديقتان»، حيث نرى رسومات أشبه بالشيفرة على الأرضية القاتمة – عصفور في شجرة، رف طيور يتحرك بخفة في السماء الليلية، قارب شراعي في مياه هادئة – كما في منمنمات عتيقة لمخطوطة مزينة، تستحضر التجانس والانسجام بين الصديقتين والطبيعة. ولكن هناك تأويلات متعددة وأسرار تدخل الحيّز – فالأولى ذات وجنتين متوهجتين وشفتين ممتلئتين منفرجتين، دلالة على إيروسها النامي الذي يضج بالتوق والتوقع ولكأنه يُضيئُها؛ أما الثانية فتقف هناك بوجه أصفر شاحب دلالة على الحضور الكلي للموت الذي يحيط بنا في زخم الحياة. يحيط بالمشهد إطار رفيع من خطوط صفراء، وكأنه بوابة أو نافذة – عالم حدودي – توقظ في الذاكرة عن بعدٍ ناءٍ الموزاييك الذهبي المتلألئ في الجوامع.

إذا كان الموضوع في كلا اللوحتين حنيناً مؤلماً، توقعاً ملءُه الأمل، ووحدة البشر، فإن هذا المزاج يبقى في المقام الأول مطبوعاً بالانسجام مع العالم المحيط. إلا أنه انسجام مع الذات التي تُبرز ماهيتها الكلية – أي «أنا كائن». – من دون ملكية دنيوية؛ إنها كائنة، لا يمكن تجاهلها، يحركها شعور رئيسي واخز بعدم الاكتفاء، بـ «لكنني لا أملك نفسي». وهذا الانسجام المشوب بالشروخ الهادئة يحوله مروان فعلاً إلى انطلاق. ولكي ينطلق في رحلته، وليتمكن من إشباع

في الشارع، ١٩٥٧.
زيت على ورق على قماش، ٢٦ × ٢١ سم.

توقه إلى ألوان الشمال وإلى أساتذة الرسم في هذا العالم الغريب، استبدله مروان بحنين أبلغ ألماً، لـ «ضياء الغسق في الشرق، على طرف البادية السورية، بلونه البرتقالي البنفسجي الزمردي الناعم».٤ ولهذا السبب على ما يبدو، ولبضع سنوات، فقد مروان كلياً هذه الـ: «أنا كائن». ولم يتبق سوى القليل من ذلك الإصرار على الانطلاق الذي كان مفعماً بالأمل والموجه كلياً نحو المستقبل، أي «نصير».

الخوف يأكل الروح

استغرق مروان بعض الوقت حتى انتقل فعلياً إلى باريس. وبعد رحلة طويلة بالسفينة حتى جنوا، ثم ملتفاً عبر مونيخ، ولنقل بالصدفة، وصل في أيلول عام ١٩٥٧ إلى برلين التي كانت آثار الحرب والدمار واضحة فيها من خلال المساحات التي ملأتها الأنقاض والحفر التي سببتها القنابل. وفي المعهد العالي للفنون

٤- عن نص دعوة مروان إلى عيد ميلاده الخامس والستين في ١٩٩٩/١/٣١.

التشكيلية، وجد في صف مدرِّسه هان ترير، الفن المعاصر ممثلاً بالتيار الألماني «اللاشكلية» informel، وبتيار الانطباعية التجريدية abstract expressionism الأمريكي، وبتيار التجريدية الغنائية abstraction lyrique الفرنسي أو البقاعية Tachisme. وهذه اللغة العالمية للفن كتوجه أسلوبي بكل ما يحمله من موقف تجاه العالم، كانت في تلك السنوات تحدد كل شيء: فهمَ الفنان لذاته، فهماً منفتحاً وشذرياً ــ من شذرة ــ للوحة، كما طبعَ صلةً بالواقع شعريةً بلا حدود حيال العالم اللاشيئي المرصود في اللوحة.

وعن طريق عفوية التدوين الإشاري الحركي للطخات، طمح هذا الفن بأدوات الرسم فحسب، المستخدمة باستقلال تام، إلى أن ينجز اللوحة المضادة التي تقدم الجواب عن العالم الداخلي غير المرئي. وكان على الحالة النفسية غير المجمَّلة للوجود الفني، بكل ما فيها من مشاعر لم تُسبر، وغير القابلة للتسمية، أن تترجَم من اللاوعي إلى حالة بصرية ذات وقع، وذلك ما أمكن، عن طريق

ديناميكية خط الرسم غير الخاضع للرقابة، وفي التوتر اللوني بين الحار والبارد
– إنه تصور لا شيئي تماماً للوحة. وقد تطلب هذا من مروان قطيعة متطرفة
مع عالم لوحته السابق، وجهداً كبيراً في العمل، يُحتمل أنه قد ارتبط بخيبة أمل
ناتجة عن فقدانه ما يمكن أن يكثف به إحساسه بالحياة بصورة مرئية
مرهفة. إلّا أنه تعلم كيف يفهم اللون من حيث قيمته الذاتية بشكل أدق، وأن
يمنحه حياته الخاصة، وأن يسيطر عليه في الوقت نفسه تدريجياً، وأن يُنطِقه
كتعبير، وفق إمكاناته الخاصة المستقلة عن الشيء، وأن يبحث في طاقة
الإيحاء المكانية للتكوينات الملونة. إن الثقافة المتحولة بشكل غير منظور في
التعامل مع اللون ستصير لاحقاً الحامل الرئيسي لفنه في الرسم – وكان هذا
هو الأمل. إنه لم ينس دمشق، لكنها صارت نائية يصعب الوصول إليها. ولكي
يؤمّن مصروفه عمل مروان في معمل للفراء نهاراً وممارسة الرسم ليلاً.

احتفظ مروان ببعض اللوحات من تلك المرحلة وأتلف المحاولات الفاشلة.
ونحو عام ١٩٦٠ كان قد توصل إلى أساس ثابت مبدئياً. وباستخدام حازم
لعدد قليل من الألوان، الأسود – الأبيض – الرمادي غالباً، والصدفي أحياناً،
اكتسبت لوحاته كثافة تصويرية لافتة، وكأن ما هو على سطح اللوحة جسم
يتوق للوجود. إن الفراغ، أو فضاء اللوحة إذا شئنا الدقة، يستولده مروان فقط
من لعبة تراكب وتداخل الألوان، وليس عبر المنظور أو التجسيد أو الانعكاس –
ومع ذلك يكاد أن يكون ملموساً ومغوياً، وهو مشهد حتماً.

ولكن هنا أيضاً: النقص المحسوس أو قصور اللوحة التجريدية: جوعه الذي
لا يُشبع نحو الانعكاس المصعَّد شعرياً للمرئي الملموس. وقد عانى بعض
زملائه من الحالة نفسها. في البداية كان الأمر نوعاً من الرفض الشبابي
العام، أي القيام بنقيض ما يمتاز به الآباء من مهارة وإتقان في عملهم. ثم
أضيف إلى الأمر أسباب أخرى، ألمانية محض، وغريبة تماماً بالنسبة لمروان.
في عام ١٩٦١ و ١٩٦٢ قام أويغن شونِبك وغيورغ بازلِيتس في البيانات
المشتركة التي اكتسبت سمعة أسطورية، والمعروفة بـ «البيانات الشيطانية
العامة» بالتعبير عن المهم الصارخ حيال العالم بحماسة عالية الحدة، فصاغا
بذلك – مدعومين شعرياً من قبل أنطونان آرتو Antonin Artaud ولوتريامون
Lautréamont- تعبيراً عن إحساس بالحياة سَيِّم جيلهم. وهو فهم للذات مأساوي
إلى حد بعيد، ومثقلٌ بأعباء التاريخ الألماني وبالشعور بالالتزام حياله، من
أجل استنهاض الذاكرة في مواجهة وعي آبائهم الغافي. وبغرض صياغة
اللوحة النقيض كجواب – رغم أمثلة فولس Wols وفوتريه Fautrier صاحب لوحات
«أوتاج» (Otages) السياسية – لم يسعفهم الفن التجريدي٥. لم يكن هذا طبعا هو
محرض مروان بطرقه الخاصة للوصول إلى لوحة تشكيلية جديدة. وهو كفرد
ضائع كان يحمل في ذاته قصة أخرى، لا تقل ثقلاً، وتوتراً مؤلماً في الروح
يطالب بتعبير مستمد من الواقع، كي يجد له حلاً ولكي يفهمه، فيتجاوز

بدون عنوان، ١٩٦٤.

تمبرا البيض– زيت على قماش، ١٠٠ × ١٢٠ سم.

الأزمة. لا شك وأنه في تلك السنين كان يعاني وحدة قارسة، وكان ممتلئاً بحنين لا يُشْبَع إلى الشعور بالاهتمام والطمأنينة وإلى وطن يأويه.

كان مروان واحد من أصدقاء الفنانين شونبك Schönebeck وبازليتس Baselitz يتناقش معهم، ويجد لديهم تفهماً لتألمه تجاه العالم، الموازي لألمهم كما يبدو، والمختلف والغريب عنه كلياً، كما وجد لديهم وجهة نظر شعرية قريبة منه – لكنه بلغته ووعيه الثقافي كان يقف خارج هذه الحلقة تماماً.

إن لوحة «تشكيل» من عام ١٩٦٣/١٩٦٤ هي مثال على هذا البحث المتلمّس والمتحوّل بين عوالم التجريد والتشكيل المتجذرة بالنسبة إليه في ثقافة مختلفة إلى حد كبير؛ وهي كمثال تشكيلي يصعب فهمها، لكنها رغم ذلك تولد تداعيات سوداء. ومن يبغي الفهم فليتذكر تلك الفتاة ذات الجسد الأصفر والضفيرة السوداء. إننا نجد هنا الموضوعَ نفسه، أفقاً ليلياً، ولكن مع شكل مستلق. إلا أن السماء هنا غير متلألئة بالنجوم، بل مدلهمة بثقل راسخ.

٥ – انظر: يورن مركرت – في مديح أويغن شونبك، خطبة في احتفال جائزة فرد تيلر للفنون التشكيلية ١٩٩٢، المعرض البرليني، برلين ١٩٩٢، ص ٤ – ٤١.

والشكل – بالأسلوب البقعي مستفيداً من إمكانات الرسم التجريدي المُنفسن – لا أكثر من كومة متداخلة من اللحم النيئ؛ جسدان بشريان ممزقان متعانقان يا ترى؟ كل شيء غامض وصامت يوحي بالتهديد؛ مثال للدمار والألم والأذى والفناء – ويذكر بشكل واهن، بظلمة ليله، بلوحات غويا الأصم السوداء. إن لوحة «بدون عنوان» من عام ١٩٦٤ تتناول الموضوعة نفسها بصورة أوضح تجسيداً على ما يبدو. فالجبل المدمى من اللحم الممزق يوحي نوعاً ما بشكل عضوي ذي شدق مفتوح عن آخره – ووحش أسطوري جانح على شاطئ مهجور ملتهم كل شيء، يتأرجح فوقه كائن خرافي في عتمة الغسق الليلي.

إذا أخذنا بعين الاعتبار ما كان سيتخذ شكلاً في عالم لوحات مروان، فلا بد من الاحتفاظ بأمرين في الذاكرة: أولهما، أن خط الرسم المجرد تماماً، الحي والعنيف الحركة والمتنوع في الوقت نفسه، لا ينسحب إلا على الأجسام الكابوسية التي ابتلعت كل ما هو حي، وحملته حرفياً ومرئياً جلياً في داخلها. والمشهدية الثانية المقابلة، أي الغسق الفضي فوق الأفق البعيد، وفوقه بقايا الليل الأسود، صامتاً تماماً، وقد رُسم درجةً لونيةً فوق أخرى، بلونية لا تكاد تتحرك، بل تتردد، ومن دون أثر للحياة.

فالجوانب المضمونية – خواءٌ يشل وجشعٌ كائن بري – تتطابق إذاً مع الموقف التعبيري لأسلوب الرسم. ثانيهما، هو التكوين غير المألوف الذي لن يعود إليه مروان لعدة عقود، لكنه سيحمل البذرة لاحقاً لبحثٍ في اللوحة سيكون مفاجئاً. وأعني تقسيم اللوحة إلى جزئين – كما في حالة انعكاس – سيُستخدمان بغرض جعل التجسيد ثنائياً. وبطريقة خاصة جداً، سينجح مروان، رغم موضوعة المشهد، في الاحتفاظ بهندسة اللوحة المسطحة الواضحة – الذي ما زال نظام اللوحة الماتيسية كامناً في خلفيته – بأسلوب متحول كلياً.

في منتصف الستينات يتوضح طريق مروان وتكتسب لوحاته وضوحاً. ففي الحلقة الواسعة للوحات الشخوص والأزواج تلتفت الآن تكوينات بشرية نحو المشاهد بمباشرة لا هوادة فيها. وجميع هذه التكوينات البشرية تقف وسط فضاءٍ خاوٍ ضاغط، انسحب منه العالم الخارجي كلياً. ومع ذلك فإنها جميعها مأزومة، لدرجة أن أجسادها، لا سيما وجوهها، تتشكل وكأنها تحت ضغط هائل. إنها صامتة كما خلف لوح زجاجي يفصلها عن العالم الخارجي بشكل عازل، تبدو وكأنها أسيرات الصمت الذي يحاول في الوقت نفسه بعدائية اختراق لفتات أجسامها التي تقارب البذاءة٦. ثمة اضطرابات سريالية تضاف إلى اللوحة بواسطة شخص ثانٍ، يبدو كشذرةٍ مقبوس، يغطيها الشخص الأول – أذرع بلا جسد تحيط بالوركين، ساق عارية لكائن غير مرئي تظهر بين ساقي الرجل، وأصبع يدٍ منبثقةٍ من الخلف تندفع نحو العين. ومع ذلك ليس ثمة ما يُحكى. البشر يصرون على صرختهم الخرساء، حتى عندما يكونون في

الواقع أزواجاً. ثمة عوالم تفصل بين لوحة الأزواج هذه، مثلاً، وبين لوحة «صديقتان» التي رسمها في دمشق قبل عشر سنوات.

لن يخطئ الإنسان النظر. فحتى إذا كانت البورتريهات الذاتية في حلقة الأعمال هذه، تحمل معنى الانعكاس – وهي ليست أقل خروجاً على الواقع من غيرها – فإن صور البشر هذه، المحمّلة بألم النبوءة المهلْوسة تجاه الواقع، ليست مجرد تأويل فرداني لذات متوحدة غريبة في كل شيء. «إنها تضم كما في بؤرة الصورة الوضع الروحي لمجتمع ما، والذي من أجله، وبقطع ساخر كأداة عرض، تُسخّر العبثية واللاواقعية اللتان يتصف بهما هذا المجتمع تحديداً».٧ – وصورة إنسان هذا المجتمع العبثية في تلك السنوات تقارب ما قدمه صموئيل بيكيت وإدوارد ألبي على خشبة المسرح.

هدية وتَحقُق

نحو عام ١٩٧٠ تمكن مروان من تحويل العالم الصارم والمضطرب درامياً لـ«تكويناته المتألمة»، (إبرهارد روترس Eberhard Roters) باتجاه أكثر هدوءاً. وفي لوحاته «وجوه مشهديّة» نجده يتحرك – مثل الكاميرا في السينما – بحيث يقترب جداً من هذه الأشكال التي تتوجه، دون افتعال، نحو الخارج، بعالمها الداخلي المليء بالعذاب. ويصير الوجه وحده، البالغ القرب، موضوع اللوحة الحميم. إلا أن هذه اللقطة القريبة التي لا يقصد بها سوى الاهتمام الفعلي والقرب، تسمح في هذه اللوحات بإبراز الحنين والسعادة والأمل من دون افتعال، وهي مشاعر منحوته في الوجوه. ويبدو أن الاستخدام السابق العنيف للروح قد انمحى تماماً أمام هذا القرب الحنون الرقيق المؤثر.

إذا كنا قد لاحظنا في مشهديات الكائنات الخرافية الدموية، تأكيد مروان على تعبيرية استخدام خطه في تشكيل الأجسام، فبإمكاننا التعرف على ما يشبه ذلك في لوحات الشخوص: فمقابل فراغ المكان الجاذِب الصامِت المثل، استُبدلت المبالغة في الإحياء بتركيز الرسم في الشخص، ولا سيما في سحنة الإنسان. إنه يسمح لنفسه الآن في لوحات «وجوه مشهديّة» – وكأنه قد تحرر – بلغة نابضة بالحركة الداخلية، بخط منساب برقة على سطح اللوحة وبتدرجات لونية ناعمة رقيقة، تغطي سطح اللوحة بكامله بتنوع بالغ التعبير. والموضوع بالنسبة إليه يشكل في الوقت نفسه ذريعة لمتابعة التوسع والتفتح في ثقافة فن رسمه. ولا شك في أنه ليس من قبيل الصدفة أبداً أن يتذكر مروان الآن تنوع سلطة تعبير التجريد، والحركة المتحولة لونياً في حركة اللاشكلية Informel التي عرفها في مرحلة الدراسة. وبحذر شديد، متلمساً طريقه، متنبهاً، ولكن بتصورات جلية رغم ذلك، يستخدم مروان اللون المحرّر من أي توصيف شيئي، كي يجعل التشكيل نابعاً من الحياة الخاصة لأدوات الرسم وحدها. يرسم السطوح بأساس شفاف ويغطيها بطبقات متعاقبة

٦ انظر مراجعتي التفصيلية لهذه المجموعة من الأعمال في: يورن مركرت – أعمال مروان المبكرة المجهولة، في كتالوغ معرض ميشائل هازنكلفر، مروان – مائيات مبكرة، مونيخ ١٩٩٠.

٧ – المرجع السابق نفسه.

بدون عنوان، ١٩٦٦.
زيت على قماش، ١٦٢ × ١٣٠ سم.

تتداخل فيها الألوان البنية المتدرجة، ونادراً ما يلجأ للأبيض أو الألوان الأساسية لإبراز أجزاء اللوحة.

كل شيء يرشح ضوءاً، الكل مشرّب بالنور، لم تعد هناك حدود ثابتة، بل تتأرجح الألوان معاً لتشكل جوهراً لونياً «حريرياً». ولهذا السبب تحديداً تصبح هذه الوجوه مشهد – مشهد للروح وللعقل. إلا أنها وبصورة مفاجئة تماماً مشهد للذكرى الحالمة، وكما تشكل الجمجمة المنتصبة عالياً الأفقَ، كذلك تذكرنا كل لوحة من هذه اللوحات، من بعدٍ وبشكل واهٍ، أيضاً، بجبل قاسيون الذي ينتصب أمام وفوق دمشق، عند الغسق بعد تراجع الحرارة ومع أوائل أضواء ليل المدينة، تندفع نسمة باردة حاملة معها لليلة المستيقظة عبق المدينة وسعادتها القريبة.

إذا كان مروان في عدد من لوحات الشخوص قد صور نفسه مراراً بصورة جلية، وإذا كانت بقية لوحات هذه المجموعة، حتى في تصعيد تعبير التشكيل، تشي عن بعدٍ ببورتريه ذاتية، فإن كل شيء في لوحات «وجوه مشهديّة» قد بدأ بالتغلغل – تشكيلٌ حر تماماً وبورتريه ذاتية حقيقية. قد يغيب التشابه كلياً أحياناً، لصالح تشكيل يلتزم فقط بالقوانين المستقلة للوحة، وبالتدقيق في إبراز تعبيرية الرسم. وعلى الرغم من ذلك يشعر المشاهد دوماً وبوضوح بأن الأمر يتعلق كل مرة بصورة واضحة لمروان نفسه، لعالمه الداخلي. لم يعد التشكيل يحتاج بعدُ إلى الانعكاس الظاهري، بل صار وعلى صعيد مختلف تماماً، فكرياً وعاطفياً، في صورة أناه.

إن اللوحة في حد ذاتها هنا تجريدية تماماً، ولهذا، إن اخترنا الدقة، ليس من الضروري أن نفتش فيها عن صورة مروان الذاتية. وفي التحول من خلال الرسم، تكتسب هذه الوجوه عموميتها، بعيداً عن أي رابط بفردانية موضوع التشكيل.

من الواضح أن مروان كان قد حضّر نفسه بشكل جيد لانطلاقته الكبرى الثانية في حياته، والتي ستنتَسِم وجوده الفني لاحقاً. فقد حصل في عام ١٩٧٣ على منحة «مدينة الفنون» Cité des Arts في باريس، ما مكّنه من تحقيق حلم شبابه الذي حمله معه عبر عشرات السنوات. وفي باريس أخيراً سيشعر باللون كهدية – ذلك اللون الذي جلبه معه من «أطراف البادية السورية» ككنز ثمين كامن في الذاكرة، من دون أن يجرؤ حتى الآن أبداً على استخدامه فعلياً – «البرتقالي الحريري، البنفسجي، الأخضر الزبرجدي». فأن يتذكرها بشوقٍ عارمٍ أمر، وأن يتمكن من رسمها أمرٌ آخر تماماً.

لكن لقاءه بالانطباعية الفرنسية – هذا الاتجاه الأسلوبي في الرسم الذي أسيء فهمه – ثم بالمعلمين القدامى، مثل فيلاسكيز المعجب به، وأخيراً بحداثة القرن العشرين الغربية، حرّره من موانع من أن يمنح نفسه كلياً لعرس اللون. فصارت لوحاته الآن أكثر حرية، مثل نوتة لحن راقص، بألوان نقية

وجه مشهدي، ١٩٧٦.

تمبرا البيض على قماش، ١٩٥ x ٢٦٠ سم.

غالباً، تعبيراً عن موسيقيةٍ بهيجة.

في«لوحات الخمار» يتناول الموضوع الذي طرقناه في البداية، موضوع الحنين إلى التورية والكشف بشكل مباشر. إنها تكتسب هنا في باريس نوعاً من الحكمة والبهجة التي تذكر بموتسارت. فتتغلغل في المشاهد عبر نحتية اللوحة وتستفزه للحوار. وكونها محجّبةٌ بغلالة خفيفة، فإنها تجذب – غالباً بمظهرها المزدوج الجنس والثنائي المعنى – وتنسحب كما في لعبة الإغواء والتمنع. شوقٌ إلى المختلف تماماً، شوقٌ نابع من الغربة، يتشرب هنا بلونية ناعمة مدمنة.

في باريس تتكثف لوحات «وجوه مشهديّة» و«لوحات الخمار» إلى أوائل لـوحـات «الـرؤوس» الـتي سـتصير عـبر السنـوات الـقـادمة ولعشرات السنين موضوعة مروان الوحيدة تقريباً. إن هذا الكنز من اللون المتحرر كلياً، أعاده معه مروان إلى برلين، بحذر وحرص من يعتني بنبتة، ويتركها عبر السنوات القادمة لتزهر بروعة خلابة. وإذا كان منذ منتصف السبعينيات قد رسم إلى

جـانب «رؤوس» «طبـيـعـة صـامـتـة» أيضـاً، أو أوائـل لوحـات «الدمى» منذ الثمانينيات، أي كلية العالم والخبرة الحياتية، فقد كان همه دائماً تشذيب الحديقة برسم مجردٍ موحٍ بالحركة، بحيث يتمكن من ترجمة الشعر الذي يـحـرك الـعـقـل والأحـاسـيـس بشكل مرئي صافٍ. ولصياغة ذلك بتنوع أكبر، كـانت مـعـالجـتـه لـلطبـيـعـة الصامتة للأشياء بمثابة أداة مهمة. فـالهدف هو إحيـاء «الميّت» بأدوات الرسم المتحررة، بحيث تتراءى دراما الإنسان مرئية عبر تجارب الحواس المؤثرة، برسم ثمرةٍ أو صينيةٍ أو إبريق، كما في لوحات سيزان Cezanne Natures mortes أو في أواني موراندي Morandi.

منذَ أن زرنا المرسم حاولنا التقاط التناقض الخاص، بأن لوحة مروان ذات تركيز هائل، أي بدقة خارقة في ما يبدو على أنه خط ريشةٍ منساباً بخفة، وأن المُشاهَدَ في الوقت نفسه معرضٌ لغواية المشاهدة الخاطفة. وليس المقصود بهذا حتماً هو المشاهدة السطحية، بل ما حددناه سابقاً، على سبيل المحاولة، بمصطلح المشاهدة الدورانية. فهنا تتعانق جوانب مختلفة من فن مروان. فمثل هذه القراءة للوحات تنسجم بدقة مع طريقة نشوئها، البالغة الأهمية في الوقت نفسه، والذي يحتاج إلى وقت طويل، فمراراً وتكراراً يعاد طلاء اللوحة، وجهاً فوق وجه، عبر السنوات، بحيث أن ما يترك مرئياً يتضمن الكثير الكثير، تماماً مثلما أن واحدنا هو نتيجة تحولات سنين عديدة.

وعلى الرغم من ذلك فإنها قابلة للتحول بين لحظة وأخرى من حيث التعبير، فتظهر وجوهاً متعددة في وجه واحد، تماماً كما في الحياة تكون لوحات مروان. كم تحتاج النبتة حتى يزهر البرعم، وبأي سرعة تذبل. ثمة توتر نجده هنا، يعبر عن إرادة مروان الفنية: المحاولة المألوفة منذ القديم لالتقاط اللحظة الأبدية بسرعة بحيث تُخلّد. وقد بدأنا الآن نفهم بشكل أفضل، ما الذي يجعل فن الرسم لدى مروان، بإيقاعه اللوني الثري الذي يتضمن في ثناياه «البرتقالي الحريري والبنفسجي والأخضر الزبرجدي» قادراً على الاحتفاظ بذكرياته المليئة بالحنين، ولماذا هي حقيقية إلى هذا الحد.

لقد خبرتُ الأمر بنفسي، عندما بدأ مروان عام ١٩٩٦ برسمي. إن فنه يـقـوم في تصويـر كل مـا هـو حـي عـلى ضـرورة التعـرف عـلى الإنسان في الانعكاس، لم يستخدمه في صوره الذاتية المبكرة فحسب، بل مارسه في

السنوات اللاحقة أيضاً – وإن شئنا الدقة، فبكثافة حتى اليوم. كانت المرة الأولى حين سنحت لي الفرصة لمراقبة مروان وهو يرسم. جلست مسترخياً، وكانت الموسيقى تصدح – عربية، كلاسيكية وقديمة من دون تمييز – وتجاذبنا أطراف الحديث، كما احتسينا الشاي. ولكن في الوقت نفسه كان التركيز مطلوباً من الموديل، أي أن يحافظ في المقام الأول على وضعيته، ولكن ليس في كل تفصيل. وبالنسبة لمروان كان الرسم فعلاً جسدياً، ليس نقل اللون، بل الرؤية المتوثبة، لا العينين فقط، بل كان عليه أن يتحرك بنفسه كثيراً بعيداً عن اللوحة، كي يحدد بدقة تظليلاً ما، نوراً ما، شكل الأنف والحاجبين. ثم كان لا بد من اختيار اللون (المناسب) – وطاولة رسمه التي تتجمع فوقها كومة ألوان إلى جانب أخرى تشكل بحد ذاتها تشتيتاً للنظر. تردد قصير، يعقبه مزج للتركيب اللوني، والنظر مجدداً، لا، اللون ليس ملائماً، مزج جديد بالريشة – ثم إن اللوحة تريد شيئاً مختلفاً تماماً، فلا يُرسم أعلى اللوحة، بل أسفلها وعلى طرفها؛ ثم يحتاج مروان للون آخر كلية. إنها لمعجزة ألا يضيع ما قد رآه مروان، بين عمليات الإدراك ومزج الألوان والتلوين. وقد يحدث هذا أحياناً، فيبدأ كل شيء من جديد. وأحياناً قد يعالج موضعاً صغيراً عدة مرات، بينما تبقى المساحات الأوسع ثابتة من المرة الأولى وحتى النهاية. خلال الاستراحات كنت أرى نفسي كل مرة بشكل مختلف، وكنت أتعرف على نفسي في كل مرة. وفي تسع جلسات، كانت تبدأ دائماً بالشك، فيما إذا كان ضرورياً تغيير شيء ما في الصورة، كانت اللوحة تتبدل كلياً، مندفعة في اتجاه مغاير تماماً. بدا الأمر كمعجزة، ارتبط بها شعور بالفقدان في الوقت نفسه، فالصيغة السابقة لم يعد بالإمكان رؤيتها مجدداً. إن البورتريه الأولى التي استغرقت

سبع جلسات رسم حتى ١٩٩٨ كانت بادىء الأمر ظاهرة شفافة وخفيفة، لوحة ذات سحر كبير، لكنها نمت من ثم إلى درجة كبيرة من التكثيف بحيث احتوت في الوقت نفسه على كثير من وجوهي، وكنت قادراً على تعرف معظمها. أما الآخرون، ومنهم أصدقاء مقربون، فإنهم يستصعبون الأمر ويحتاجون إلى وقت أطول؛ فلربما كانوا يعرفون لي وجوهاً أخرى، قد لا تكون تلك التي يعرفها مروان. يبقى الأمر مدعاة للدهشة أن ينجح مروان في بورتريهاته، على الرغم من الشبه بين الموضوع

يورن ميركيرت، ١٩٩٨.
زيت على قماش، ١٤٦ × ٢٢٨ سم.

٢٥

والانعكاس، بالحفاظ على استقلالية أسلوبه وأن يجعل الشكل ينمو منها بكل دقة ولكأن الأمر محض صدفة.

ثمة أمر آخر يرتبط بفن مروان المتناقض من حيث تعدد طبقاته الزمنية؛ وهو ما يمكن فهمه أيضاً من خلال القول مرة ثانية بتجذره إنسانياً: إنها نوعية الظاهرة الخاصة بكافة لوحاته، ولا سيما بالوجوه والرؤوس. وهو أمر يقترب من المقدس – لكنه في الوقت نفسه يتصف بحداثة كبيرة تكاد أن تكون يائسة. وأفضل مثال لإدراك ذلك هو جياكومتّي Giacometti الذي يعالج في جميع منحوتاته المعاصرة جداً، أي إنهاء المنظور، قضية التداخل بين ما هو ناءٍ وما هو قريب جداً. فعن بعد أرى الشكل جلياً وواضحاً، ولكن من دون تفاصيل، أما عن قرب فإني أرى كل جزء بدقة متناهية، لكني أفقد رؤية الشكل بكليته. وواقع الحال أن الإنسان الذي يريد جياكومتي أن يقدم لنا صورة عنه يتشكل من البعدين في إدراكنا. وهكذا هناك أشكال ضئيلة الحجم تبدو للمشاهد عن قرب شديد بالغة البعد عنه؛ وهناك أشكال هائلة الحجم توحي للمشاهد بنظرة قريبة على الرغم من بعدها الشديد عنه.

والأمر مشابه تماماً في ما يتعلق بلوحات «الرؤوس» مروان. فهو أيضاً يرسم حجوماً ضئيلة وعملاقة – بالكثافة والقوة نفسها، وبنفس تنوع اللا محدود للتعبير؛ وهناك دائماً ذلك التزامن المتناقض الذي يجمع القريب والبعيد. وتحديداً في الرؤوس المرسومة دائماً من نظرة قريبة جداً، والتي تزداد قرباً من المشاهد عبر السنوات بطريقة لا تصدق، نجد أنفسنا أمام الظاهرة نفسها. ولأنها بالتحديد لم (تُرسم)، وإنما لأنها نشأت من خط الرسم التجريدي بطريقة طبيعية غير قسرية، فإننا لا نستطيع التعرف عليها بوضوح تام إلا عندما نقترب منها عن مسافة بعيدة. عندها يتبدى القرب الهائل في تعبير اللوحة التي لا تشتمل على الرأس أصلا إلا من لقطة قريبة جداً. فإذا اقترب المشاهد منها، تحللت تدريجياً واستعصت على أي إدراك. وفي مقابل ذلك ينفرش أمام العين حقل التلوينات الجزئية الثمينة التي تخفي في كل تفصيل القرب الذي شوهد للتو، وهو الحقل المشع، المضيء، المتلألئ، المزهر والذابل. ولهذا ينجح مروان في لوحاته بأكثر من أن يعكس الإنسان فحسب، ولهذا تعلق في شبكة اللون الحسية وخطها المنداح كتابةً كافة الذكريات والأشواق واليأس واليقين. وهكذا نلتقي في هذه اللوحات فعلياً بامتلاك العالم في الصيرورة، حسب إرنست بلوخ. «أنا كائن. لكنني لا أملك نفسي. ولهذا فإننا نصير».

بين عالمين

لقد أسعفني الحظ بمرافقة مروان في بعض رحلاته إلى دمشق وعبر سوريا، وإلى عمان وعبر الأردن. على الرغم من نشاط وسرعة إيقاع المدن الحديثة هناك وناسها، كنت أفلح دائماً في التقاط آثار عالم مروان الماضي، والذي ما

زال يحمله حياً وحيوياً في نفسه كي يبقى في صورة الإنسان. في أحد نصوصي حول مروان كتب لي أستاذي القديم فرنر هافتمن: ... هذا كله صحيح جداً: جواب هذا السوري المرهف بلغة أوربية على ما يحمله في ذاته – البـاروك والصـحـراء. يضـاف إلى ذلك وحـدة حسـيـة الإنسـان البـدوي «...كالحلزونة تحمل بيتها على ظهرها وتترك آثارها على الطمي...» ٨ قول صائب تماماً، لكنه لا ينطبق فقط على عالم لوحات مروان. فطريق حياته الممتد بعيداً قد سلخه أيضاً عن موطنه البيوغرافي (السِيَري) – وهل كان للأمر أن يكون على غير ذلك. عندما يكون مع أصدقائه وزملاء يفاعته ومع العائلة، عندها يُحتضن بفرح وسعادة كابن ضائع. ولكن حتى تجاه الأكثر قرباً منه، يحمل في نفسه شيئاً غريباً تجاهه. فهو الذي خرج إلى العالم، ولم يعد إلى الوطن إلا لفترة قصيرة. إنه بروحه البدوية المرهفة قد حمل إلى العالم الغريب في الخارج وأدخل في الفن الغربي شعوراً شرقياً بالحياة؛ إنه متمكن من الفن الأوربي – وبالتحديد أيضاً تجاه الأفق المجيد لفن الرسم الثمين – بشكل فريد، لكنه كان دائماً يتحدث بثقة عميقة عن عجائب ذلك العالم الذي

الصديق، ٢٠٠٤.

زيت على قماش، ٨٩ x ١٣٠ سم.

أتى منه. ولهذا فإنهم يحترمونه بامتنان؛ ولهذا أيضاً صار في الوقت نفسه بالنسبة لهم غريباً. فليس من السهل على الأصدقاء العرب التعرف على مألوفهم في لغة غريبة. لا يوجد في العالم العربي المعجب بعمله بعمله أي أثر لتلك الغربة التي يشعر بها مروان في نفسه في أوربا التي تُشعره بها أحياناً. الأمر في برلين مختلف طبعاً، وكذلك في باريس حيث يحظى بالتقدير العالي من معهد العالم العربي حتى المكتبة الوطنية؛ إنهم هناك يحبون غربته، على هذا الوجه وذاك.

إن مروان هو المعلم الذي صار، آتياً من الغربة، والذي بقي غريباً في العالم. لقد أهدانا جميعاً لوحات ثمينة، تحمل في طياتها أحلامنا الخاصة جداً عن الحياة، بشكل نموذجي – بسحر يأخذ بنا جميعاً، بسحر خرافي يوقظ الذاكرة، مترع بالحنين وبالمواساة.

٨– تبليغ شخصي من فرنر هافتمن إلى المؤلف بتاريخ ١٩٧٧/١/١٩، مقبوس عن: يورن مركرت – «خدُوج Kadousch» أو تحولات شذرات أفكار حول لوحات مروان، في: كتالوغ معرض اتحاد الفن، دارمشتت، برلين ١٩٨٤، ص ١٩.

ترجمة: د. نبيل الحفار

راجعها مروان

صفحة ٣٠. رأس، ١٩٩٥.
آكريل – زيت على ورق، ١٥٢ x ٢٢٢ سم.
مجموعة خالد وسهى شومان، عمّان

صفحة ٣١. رأس، ١٩٩٦.
زيت على قماش، ١٦٢ x ١٣٠ سم.
مجموعة خالد وسهى شومان، عمّان

إنعكاس، ١٩٩٧–١٩٩٨.
زيت على قماش، ١٩٥ x ٢٦٠ سم.

يوآخيم سارتوريوس
مروان ومشهد الأسئلة النهائية

اللوحة الأولى التي نعرفها لمروان والتي رسمها في دمشق، في الثالثة عشرة من عمره، تعود إلى العام ١٩٤٧، وتمثل منظراً طبيعياً أمام أبواب مدينته الأم. تتميّز هذه اللوحة المتأثرة بالإنطباعية الفرنسية بحرية مدهشة في لمساتها.

الآن، يعمل الرسام في مرسمه في برلين على لوحة داكنة تمثل رأسين متساندين. وها نحن نحتفل بانطلاقه المثابر على طريق يشقها منذ حوالى خمسين سنة.

ماذا أقصد من كلمة (مثابر)؟ أقصد أنّه حقق في النصف الثاني من القرن الأخير المنصرم، بدءاً من ١٩٥٣ إنتصارات متجددة لفن الرسم الذي أعلن مراراً عن نهايته والذي زاحمته باستمرار تقنيات أخرى في التشكيل. وهي إنتصارات أنجزها برؤية تختلف اختلافاً جلياً عن تلك التي صدر عنها الواقعيون والتجريديون والبنائيون أو الإنشائيون. أقصد كذلك من كلمة (مثابر) أن مروان عاش هذه الفترة كلها في بحث دائم عن طرق تشكيلية تتيح له أن يفصح بالرسم عن قضايا وجودية. يتضح ذلك بمجرد إطلالة على مجمل أعماله: مجموعة المناظر الطبيعية المبكرة، الأشخاص الذين يتأرجحون بين التجريد والتشخيص، الأزواج، الرؤوس الكبيرة، مجموعة الوجوه المعذبة، الدمى، لوحات الطبيعة الصامتة، الرؤوس التذكارية العملاقة، ثانية، و(الرؤوس المزدوجة) أخيراً.

مرة، قال لي مروان في مرسمه: (لوحاتي عُمقياً وجودية)، ثم أردف قائلاً «اللوحة شبيهةٌ بالجرح». الأرجح أن مروان ينطلق، بحثاً عن موضوعات للوحاته، من حقائق واقعية. ولا يعبر رسمه عن مجرد حالة إنفعالية. إنه يعرف، على نحوٍ عالٍ، أن لغة الشعر التي يجيدها في صورة مدهشة، والتي

يستخدمها صديقه الشاعر الكبير أدونيس للتعبير عن قلق الإنسان وبؤسه، تختلف عن لغة الرسم. فما أصعب أن يعبر المرء عن الفقدان في لوحة، وأن يظهر العذاب من وراء الخطوط، أو أن يرسم صمت آلاف السنين.

دائما، يربط مروان بين عمل الرسام وعمل المهندس المعماري. كل لوحة تتطلب منه وقتاً طويلاً، حتى أنه لم ينجز في السنوات الأخيرة إلا أربع لوحات أو خمساً في السنة يعدها (منتهيه)، حقاً.

وهو يضع الألوان طبقةً فوق أخرى، بدأبٍ وتكثيفٍ كبيرين، كما لو أن التجارب في أثناء ذلك تترسب وتتراكم. ولقد حاولت أن أعبر عن ذلك في قصيدة كتبتها حول عمله قائلاً:

ليس هناك إلا وجهْ
يُبنى ويُهدم ويُعاد بناؤه
مرتعشاً،
يتقلب بين الموت والحياة،
لهذا، يبدو فجأةً
كأنه وجه لا يمحى.

في لوحاته التي رسمها في السنوات الأخيرة، تتموضع طبقات اللون بكثافة عالية، وتسيل تحت أحمرها القاني قنوات زرقاء خضراء، وينبثق الأصفر من كوى شهباء سوداء، وتتماوج ظلالٌ سمراء منكسرة ومتداخلة. إنها لوحات تذكرني تحديداً بتخيل الإسلام لنشأة الإنسان من علق من تراب ثم يأخذ في النمو متدرجاً في أشكالٍ عديدة، وصولاً إلى هيئته الأخيرة.

إن مروان رسام – رسام قبل أي شيء آخر، وباستمرار. ولا يهتم في الأخير، ما تكون القصة التي تولّدت عنها لوحته، أو ما يكون دافعها الأساسي، سواء اتصل الأمر بحجاب المرأة في دمشق، أو بفلسطيني مقتول بين ذراعي صديقه. ذلك أن المهم يتمثل في العلاقات ما بين حقول الألوان وشرائحها، والألق – داكناً يسبح في النور، وينكسر فائضاً علينا. لا يُدرك المرء أن للألوان في الرسم بعداً فيزيائياً ونفسياً في آن، كما يُدرك ذلك عند مروان. حتى ما سماه (تشخيصات) في أواخر الستينات، وهي أعمال واقعية، نسبياً، لا نجد فيها بحثاً عن صورة تطابق الأصل، وإنما نجد بحثاً في الأشياء عن حقيقتها التصويرية. وهذا يعني، وفقاً للعمل الشاق في نشوء اللوحة، أن جانباً من وجود الفنان يتجسد في كل لوحة، تجسداً ملموساً. إن جميع لوحاته، وبخاصة تلك التي أنجزها في السنوات العشر الأخيرة، لغات مكثفة عاطفياً، وتكاد، تبعاً لذلك، أن تكون مجردة، تفصح عن معاناة الوجود البشري، مليئة بجمر الألم، وصدمة المعرفة، وجراح الحب. ولو طلب مني أن أذكر أسلافاً لفن مروان لذكرت في المقام الأول أنطونان آرتو برسومه (البورتريهات) الخالدة التي صور فيها نفسه وآخرين، والتي أنجزها في «مصح رودن». فهي قائمة على

التوازن نفسه، بين النشوة والإضمحلال، مما نراه عند مروان. كنت ذكرت كذلك إدوار مونش وفان غوغ لبصيرتهما التصويرية التي عبر كل من منهما، بطريقته الرؤيوية الخاصة، عما عرفه عن الإنسان ووجوده، وألبرتو جياكوميتي للتطابق في عمله الفني بين القرب والبعد، ذلك أن الوجه في عمل مروان يتداعى عند الإقتراب، فيتحول إلى نوع من لعب حر للألوان. كنت ذكرت أخيراً مارك روثكو الذي تفرد في القدرة على التعبير عن التأمل والهدوء والإنطواء. غير أن مروان لا يقاسم روثكو هيبته، فلوحاته هجومية، على رغم إنزوائها التأملي، وتكاد الرؤوس الضخمة التذكارية عنده أن تشبه الأيقونات، والوجه الإلهي، ومحور الأرض، مما يصلها بباطنية روثكو. هذا ما أراه، على الأقل. ونجد أخيرا، عند كليمها صمتاً للكون لا يكاد أن يطاق.

قبل سنوات، أصغيت إلى حديث بين هاينر مولر ويانيس كونيليس في (باب باريس) ببرلين، وكان يدور حول المقومات التي ينهض عليها الفن الكبير. وعليّ هنا أن أشير إلى أن مولر لم يكن يجيد الإنكليزية، وأن كونيليس لا يجيد الإيطالية ولا اليونانية. هكذا استخدما الإيماء ضاحكين ورسما رسوماً صغيرة على مناديل الورق واستخدما الأصابع والأيدي التي كانا يضعانها على آذانهما بين وقت وآخر. كانت خلاصة هذا الحوار الفريد أن (الفن الكبير) هو الذي يوحد بين اللغة الكونية والعناصر المحلية الأصلية والذاتية. وقد سئل مروان كثيراً عن تأثير وطنه سورية، التي كانت في العصور القديمة إنتهاء بالفترة العثمانية ملتقى مفتوحاً بين بلاد فارس والأناضول ومصر والبحر الأبيض المتوسط مكونة بوصفها كذلك، قطباً وضاد لبرلين – المكان الشمالي غير المريح الممزق البارد الذي وجد فيه مروان الطفل مأوى ومكاناً يعجان بالأشياء المحسوسة. وهو يتحدث عن ذلك بحماسة، فيذكر ضوء المساء البنفسجي وأزيز الطائرات الورقية في السماء، والضوء الزمرّدي الذي يتسرب من الأشجار إلى ساحات البيوت، والنساء اللاتي كن يثرن شهوة الصبي المراهق. ويفصح عن هذا كله بحساسية شرقية كاملة – كما نلحظها في السجاد، وتلوين المخطوطات المصورة النفيسة، إضافة إلى فسيفساء الجامع الكبير في دمشق بألوانه الذهبية والداكنة. وأعترف أنني أتساءل عما نجد من هذا كله، في صورة ملموسة، في لوحات مروان.

لقد درس مروان الأدب العربي في جامعة دمشق بين ١٩٥٥ و ١٩٥٧. وفي أيلول من هذا العام الأخير نفسه، جاء إلى برلين، ليدرس عند هان ترير في أكاديمية الفنون، حاصراً اهتمامه، إلى فترة، باتجاه (المدرسة البقعية). وأعلن في أثناء إقامة له بباريس في السنة ١٩٧٣ في إطار منحة دراسية عن حبه لبهاء الألوان الزاهية، بوصفها تراثاً عربياً كان حياً في نفسه، قبل ذلك، منذ بداياته. فلئن كانت دمشق حاضرة في أعماله كلها، بوصفها رمزاً، فإنها تشكل في لوحته إيماءها الروحي، أو بنيتها الخفية أو الخط الدفين فيها – أو

رأس، ١٩٩٧.

زيت على قماش، ٢٦٠ x ١٩٥ سم.

تشكل نوعاً من الإستشراف. لكن، ماذا عن لغة الكون التعبيرية؟ كان الرأس، من هذه الناحية، العنصر الثابت في فن مروان، طول نصف قرنٍ كامل. ويمكن، بدلاً من الرأس، أن نقول: الوجه. الرأس بالنسبة إلى مروان، مشهد الأسئلة النهائية. الأجزاء الثلاثة لإحدى أهمّ الروايات في القرن العشرين. عنيت «الإنبهار»، لإلياس كانيتي مُعَنْوَنَه تباعاً كما يلي: «رأس دون عالم، عالم دون رأس، العالم في الرأس».

يـتخيل مروان الرأس عـالماً، ومشهداً للروح، ودائرةً تنطوي عـلى الكون، ومكاناً للعذاب والكآبة والحب. ذلك أن العيون أكانت ببؤبؤٍ أم من دونه، تتجه دوماً نحو الداخل. هكذا تتوهج وتصد في آن. وقد كوّن مروان هذه الفكرة الرئيسية ونوّع عليها، طول عقود كثيرة. وهي تعكس على رغم كونها محدودة، إمكاناته الفنية كلها، وتبلغ ذروتها في متواليته: (٩٩ وجهاً) تلك السلسلة من الأوراق الغرافيكية التي لا مثيل لها والتي نستطيع أن نسميها بحق خلاصة لجميع ابتكارات مروان التصويرية في مجال يتقنه إتقان المعلم. كان مروان يعرض هنا حالات الإنسان النفسية الأساسية بعد أن انعكست في آلاف المرايا أو كأنه يحكيها في آلاف القصص الرمزية لكي يخلص إلى الكلام الصحيح عن الهشاشة والخوف والخفر، لكن إضافة إلى الثقة بالنفس، والتضامن بلا تحفظ. تظل حيوية الوجوه التي يرسمها تدهش دائماً من ينظر إليها، فالوجه عنده يمثل الشخص كله، وفي ما وراءه، الإنسان.

ينبغي، في هذا السياق، أن نتذكر أن الرأس موضوع رئيس في فن القرن العشرين. يكفي أن نشير إلى رؤوس برانكوزي وآرشيبنكو وهانس أولمان أو هورست أنتيس كانت الصورة المجردة غير المثالية والتي لا تدل على شخص بعينه نتيجةً لتطور طويل بدأ حوالي ١٨٩٠، عندما تحرر فن التصور من وظيفة التقليد مركزاً على صياغات معممة للرأس، وأدى ذلك إلى الصورة التكعيبية، التي تتصف بإسلوب متصاعد يلغي جذرياً وظيفة البورتريه التقليدية، مما لم يكن متخيلاً قبل ذلك. مثل تلك الرؤوس، وبينها الرؤوس المتنامية الضخامة عند مروان، إنما هي في الأخير صياغات فنية لا تمارس فعلها إلا في المجال الجمالي. وهي هنا مشحونة بدلالة مختلفة تماما، تصل إلى مستوى السحرية والباطنية، كما هي الحال عند مروان. أفلا نبحث جميعاً عن تجسيد، وعن مجازٍ قوي؟ وهذا ما يجده مروان في الرأس ويجد فيه العالم. هكذا لا يرسم الرأس لوجه الرأس بل لهاجس عميق جارف يحثه على إظهار العالم وتفسيره فهو يعمل على أن يقدم عن العالم الوصف الأكثر كثافة، عبر عودته المستمرة إلى الرؤوس، بعد المرور في موضوعات أخرى، كما نرى في أعمال الطبيعة الصامتة المتلألئة التي تعيش فيها الأشياء حياة مستقلة ودرامية، وفي الدمى المتحركة التي تشكل مشهداً لفن شامل من الرسم المتحرر على صعيد الأحاسيس. يقرر مروان موضوعه، مكراراً العالم. وعندما ننظر إلى

هذه الرؤوس طويلاً ونتفتح لها لكي تتفتح لنا، ندخل إلى برزخ يقع بين صمت قديم قِدم العصور، وحزن يصرخ دون أن يحدث أي صوت. ولعل ذلك ما أراد الشاعر الأميركي كليتون اشيليمان أن يشير إليه في قصيدته عن (وجوه) مروان، إذ يقول:

« (...) في برزخ بيننا
ليس نقطة غيبيّةً
بل عمق بين الجلد المسلوخ
وقناع الموت الخَفي ».

أن ذلك البرزخ – «يـفصـح عـن توتـر، أو لـنقل عـن إزدواجيـة «أو ثنائية» موجودة في أعمال مروان عبر مراحله الإبداعية كلها، وقد لفت نـظـري ذلك «البرزخ» في أعمـال مروان عندما شاهدتها للمرة الأولى في قاعة العرض في مدينة بون، سنة ١٩٧٣. كان المعرض يضم المشاهد الوجهية الكبيرة، إضافةً إلى رؤوس عريضة ترقد على الوسائد بارزةً بين الملاءات، وعلى بـعضها خمارٌ في مـنـتـهـى الشفافية. إنهم شخوصٌ معزولون وخجولون بهويات معقدة. وقـد شعرت بـأن هـذه اللـوحـات مـرسـومـة بـغضب مـرهـف، فيما تتأرجح بين التذكير والتأنيس، بين الجلاء والخفــاء، بين الخوف مـن الـوحـدة والـرغـبـة فيهـا. ولا تـزال لـوحـات مروان تـنـهض على هـذه الثنائية. كانت هذه الثنائية في بـعض مـراحـل إبداعـه جـزءاً مـن موضوع اللوحة ومن بنيتها. فقد أنجز في سنتي ١٩٦٣–١٩٦٤ عدة لوحات تتكون كل منها من هيئتين لا شكل لهما، كمثل أجسام جرفت إلى شاطئ رمادي أمام سماء سوداء، في

بدون عنوان، ١٩٦٤.
تمبرا البيض – زيت على قماش، ١٢٠ X ١٠٠ سم.

جوٌّ رصاصي. الآن، تظهر من جديد هذه الثنائيات في شكل لوحاتٍ كبيرة الحجم، يظهر في كل منها وجهان أحدهما فوق الآخر، كما لو أنهما ينعكسان على سطح ماءٍ يفصل بينهما، أو يظهران متلاصقين أحدهما إلى جانب الآخر، ويكون أحد الرأسين، أحياناً، معكوساً، مستنداً إلى الآخر. وقد أعطى مروان لهذه الرؤوس المزدوجة عنوان «الصديق»، في إشارة أحياناً إلى الغياب. الوجه الأمامي الذي يواجهنا ملون بألوان كثيرة تتكون من ظلال دافئة لا تحصى: قرمزية، صفراء، برتقالية، رملية. وجميعها مختصرة تحرك فضاء اللوحة، وتمنحه إيقاعاً يتدفق حول سيرها: الوجه الثاني. وهذا الأخير خافت اللون، رمادي مع ميل إلى الأبيض والأخضر. أو هو، بالأحرى، رمز للموت الذي تعانقه الحياة وتسنده. قد يكون ذلك غريباً، لكنني لم أقدر أمام تلك الرؤوس «الميتة» إلا أن أحدس بحدس وجه المسيح، مطبوعاً على غطاء الموت الكتاني: «فيرونيكا»، وصور العذراء «بييتا» القروسطية (...) في البشر ضعفٌ، وهذا نقص. غير أنه نقص شقيق للشوق، وهو لذلك يمنحهم القوة. وتتضح تلك القوة مباشرة عبر الوجه الجبهي، والجبين المرتفع، والفم الصلب، وهي تتغلب على ذلك النقص، مشيرة إلى شيء لا يغلب، كما لو أن الشخص لا يموت إلا لكي يبعث في شخص آخر. فلا يمكن أن نفهم لوحات هذه المرحلة الأخيرة في معزل عن بعدها الميتافيزيقي، حيث الوجه وفقاً لتعبير أدونيس:

« طاقة إشعاع،

تتموج في فضاء النظر،

كما لو أن المرئي هو، تحديداً، ما لا نراه ».

إن فن مروان مغامرة روحية. وبين أسلافه، في هذه المغامرة فنانون كبار: بونار، بيكاسو، روثكو، وقد تقدم مروان في الجرأة، طرداً مع تقدمه في العمر، فهو يصنع من كوكبه من الألوان، والنقاط العابرة، والخطوط، والكتابة الإيمائية المرتجلة، كثافة تزداد مع تحولات الوجه التي تتعاقب كلما ازددنا منه قرباً. وتمثل هذه الكثافة المتوهّجة المرتعشة توفيقاً بين الأنا والعالم، وبين المرئي واللامرئي. ماذا أقصد؟ أقصد أن مروان رسام أولاً وأخيراً. غير أنه، إلى ذلك، متصوف ينهل في آن من التراثين الغربي والعربي، وفي ذلك ما يضفي على لوحاته جمالاً داخلياً. وليس السحر هنا جامداً، ففي هدوء لوحاته نشعر بالحركة، ونحس بقربها الحميم إلى الشعر، بوصفها تظهر الخفي. يعمل أثر اليد على الوصول إلى صوت القلب، ويعمل صوت القلب على الإفصاح عن إيقاع العالم.

في تكريم مروان ٢٠٠٢
نقلها عن اللغة الألمانية غوتر أورت
راجعها أدونيس

روبرت كودييلكا

مروان يرسم بورتريه

قبل ما يزيد عن عامين قال مروان إنه يريد رسم صورة بورتريه لي. موافقتي على ذلك أظهرت لي مرة أخرى ما يمكن إيلاؤه من قيمة لقناعاتنا الثابتة، لأنني في الواقع لا أحب صوري. فعندما أنظر في الصباح الباكر في المرآة أتأسف أحياناً على التخلف الذكوري في مضمار الحياة الاجتماعية، وبالطبع لا تكون الصدمة عند المرأة أقل عندما تعجز في تلك اللحظة الأولى من مواجهة الذات وبصورة غير متوقعة عن أن تتعرف على نفسها. الأمر هو كمثل الذي يكون على سفر فيستيقظ في غرفة في أحد الفنادق ولا يعرف للوهلة الأولى أين هو. الفارق الوحيد هو أن المكان الذي يصعب تحديده هو وجه الإنسان نفسه. إلا أن النساء يعرفن، أو يتعلمن كثيرا في وقت مبكر، أن هذه الحالة ليست واقعاً قائماً، وإنما مهمة تفرض إجراء ترميم صارم لصورة الذات المشتتة ليلاً، وإعادة تصويبها نحو الذات الداخلية ونحو الآخرين حفاظا على ذلك القناع الموحد الآمن الذي لا يمكن بدونه التواصل الصريح بين الناس.

ما يدهشني كل صباح هو رؤية الفتيات اللواتي يجلسن على عتبات الدار التي أسكنها بالأجرة، وهن يتلذذن بنهم بالسيجارة الأخيرة قبل أن يتحركن بخطى متثاقلة إلى المدرسة القريبة. طويلات القامة أم قصيرات، نحيفات أم بدينات، هن مثل سرب الطيور، يصعب على الواحد منا تمييزهن من وجوههن التي تحمل علامات التجميل العصرية المميزة للفتيات.

عدم النجاح في التعرف المباشر على الذات في المرآة لا يساوي بالطبع شيئا مقارنة بالحيرة التي توقعني فيها الصور الفوتوغرافية. فأنا لا أفهم ببساطة أولئك الذين يعرضون على بعضهم البعض مثل هذه الصور ويقولون بانفعال مشيرين بأصابعهم إلى موقع معين: أترى، هناك في الخلف، هذا أنا.

عبد الرحمن منيف، ١٩٩٦.

ما أراه في مثل هذه اللقطات دوما عينين لا يظهران إلا بالكاد من خلف أجفان مسبلة أو فما مفتوحا حتى الأشداق، أو ضحكة تُظهر أسنانا براقة أو قسمات وجه تُظهر ضجر من ضُبط شاردا. مثل هذه الفلتات ليست غريبة علي، فجيزيلا تقول أحيانا عندما أكون في الغالب أفكر أو أحاول تتبع ما تقوله بانتباه: لا تنظر عابساً هكذا. لكن تثبيت هذه الانفعالات اللاإرادية في لقطة ما تؤدي غالبا إلى مبالغة رهيبة: كما لو أن مجنونا دخـل غـاليري الحيـاة الملتقطـة في صـور. التشخيص موضوعي ومؤكد اكثر من مرة. قبل فترة قصيرة قالت لي مصورة صحفية قُدّمت إليها على أنني شخصية مهمة وهي تريني أول صورة التقطتها لي:«إنك لا تبدو مثل هذه الصورة السيئة، علينا أن نلتقط صورة أخرى.»

حسنا هذا يكفي، ما عددته من تحفظات لا يرمي سوى إلى إظهار أن تلبيتي لرغبة مروان في رسم صورة بورتريه لي ، غير المبررة إطلاقا بالمناسبة، لم تكن من باب الغرور أو من باب الرغبة في الخلود، فأنا فعلا لا أحب صوري. لكن إغراء القدوم المنتظم لبعض الوقت إلى مرسمه في شارع شمارغن دورف بمنأى عن عبء النصوص والمشاريع وما شابه ذلك من قيود الواجبات كان قويا جدا.

عزّة منيف، ١٩٩٩.

بالنسبة لي كان مرسم مروان العتيق منذ رؤيتي له في العام ١٩٨٢ على الدوام واحة حضارة في برلين. إلى جانب ذلك، وإضافة إليه، كان هناك طبعا دافع آخر. إذ أن فن البورتريه يبدو في الظاهر أبسط أنواع التصوير لكنه في الواقع أكثرها عمقاً، ذلك لأن بعده الفني لا يظهر إلا بعد زوال الغاية المباشرة منه، أي عندما يموت صاحب الصورة أو يُنسى وتزول بذلك إمكانية التأكد من وجود الشبه بين الصورة والأصل. وشهرة رسامي البورتريه الكبار من أمثال هولباين وتيتزيان أو ريمبرانت تقوم أساساً على خلود الصور التي رسمت بتكليف وبنية الصمود أمام المقارنة بالأشخاص الأحياء. إننا نؤمن بثبات بمعرفتنا بشكل ما بالأشخاص في الصور، ولكن من الذي نعرفه أو ما الذي نعرفه في جهلنا؟ يحكي بول فاليري عن صديق قال بعفوية أمام بورتريه ديكارت التي رسمها فرانس هالز إن الصورة شبيهة جدا به. وبالفعل توحي الخصلات الملتصقة بخفة على الجبين

والأكياس الغائرة تحت عيني مدخن الجيتان بذلك الشبه. إلا أن فاليري يسأل بدقة وبنبرة ذات مغزى: شبيهة بمن؟.

ليس فقط من باب الصداقة بل أيضا بشيء من الفضول لمعرفة ما إذا كانت ملامسة ذلك الشبه والمرء على قيد الحياة ممكنة بسرعة. توجهت صيف عام ٢٠٠٢ لأصعد الدرج في شارع شمارغن دورف مارا بلوحات وإعلانات الشركات الصغيرة الأخرى، وعادة تحسّن أسماء الشركات مزاجي، بالإضافة إلى ذلك كان الموعد دوما بعد الظهر في تلك الساعة التي وصفها نيتشه بأنها الفترة التي يضعف فيها عنفوان النهار ويلين الضوء. لدى وصولي كان الباب غالبا مفتوحا في انتظاري ومروان كان يعد القهوة العربية لي. وكنّا دائما نُؤخّر بدء العمل قليلا. فبداية كنت أعجب بالنظر من النافذة الشمالية الكبيرة فوق سطوح منازل المدينة مرورا بأشجار الروبينيا وليس الأكاسيا كما صحح لي مروان. أما هو فكان يتذكر بداياته في هذا المكان. بعد ذلك كان كل منا يأخذ مكانه، فكنت أجلس على كرسي محدد مكانه سلفا أمام الجدار الغربي للمرسم والذي كان يرسم عليه عادة الصور الكبيرة. أمامي على اليمين وعلى خط موارب يبعد ثلاثة أمتار كنت أرى ظهر الحامل، وأمامي على اليسار وعلى

روبرت كودييلكا (حالة)، ٢٠٠٢.

زيت على قماش، ٨٩ × ١٣٠ سم.

مسافة أكبر من المسافة السابقة بمقدار النصف تقريبا كانت طاولة الرسم، وكان مروان يتحرك في المسافة الخالية بين هذين الموقعين.

اكتشفت منذ الجلسة الأولى شيئا مذهلا، فتسهيلا للجلوس بسكون بدأت أثرثر بحرية وحبور ومروان مستمع رائع يعطي محدثه شعورا بتبادل الحديث من خلال موافقة شامتة أو ابتسامة مسامحة أو بآهة مقاطعة، وفي الوقت الذي ركّز فيه كامل انتباهه إلى التنقل بين طاولة الرسم والقماش ووجهي، حوّلت نظري ببطء نحو الأسفل فرأيت ما لم أكن أتوقعه: كان مروان ينتعل حذاء رياضيا، ليس كالأحذية الرياضية العادية وإنما من ماركة عالمية مشهورة، وطبعا باستطاعة كل من يعجب بهذه الأحذية انتعالها ولكن المفاجأة تمثلت في الخفة والخطوات الواثقة التي كان مروان يتحرك بها بما يتناسب مع الحذاء الرياضي على قدميه.

لم تنقشع الغشاوة عن عيني إلا في الجلسة الثانية فما كان يجري بين طاولة الرسم والقماش لم يكن سوى نسخة أخرى من رقصة الملاكم الشهير محمد علي الذي كان يرقص كالفراشة ويلسع كالنحلة. وذلك بالتطابق الكامل في حركة الساقين مع الملاكم العظيم، بغض النظر عن التشبيه غير الكامل. فالفراشات لا ترقص، بل هي تطير وتتهادى وتترنح في الهواء، أما مروان فكان يرقص مثل بطل العالم نفسه: خطوتان أو ثلاث إلى الأمام بخفة نحو القماش ومن ثم خطوة جانبية لالتقاط منظر الموديل ولموازنة الحركة وفي الختام ضربة الفرشاة المخربشة على القماش والعودة بنصف دائرة على العقبين تقريبا إلى طاولة الرسم والإعداد من جديد عبر تنظيف الفرشاة وتغيير اللون وإضافة صبغة جديدة عليه، ومن ثم نظرة قصيرة للقماش والموديل للتأكد قبل بدء الهجوم الجديد بخطوتين أو ثلاث إلى الأمام. هكذا كانت تمر الساعة أو ما يزيد عنها دون قياس، وكنا نمضيها معا بجولة طويلة مليئة بالحركة السريعة في البداية وأخرى قصيرة وهادئة، وبين الجولتين كانت هناك فرصة نحاول خلالها تبادل حديث هادئ، أثناء تناولنا الشاي أو القهوة بالهال دون أن نكثر من استراق النظر إلى حالة الصور.

ورغم ذلك أصبح السؤال عن الصورة الختامية لرقصة مروان أكثر إلحاحا مع مرور الوقت: فهل كان الراقص المتحرك في المثلث بين طاولة الرسم والقماش والموديل يلسع أيضا كالنحلة؟ بعد الجلسة الأولى سجلت بنوع من الارتياح أن نسيج البقع المبعثرة لم يكن يُظهر أي شبه واضح مع أي شخص بالنسبة لي. إلا أن ذلك تغير مع تكثف شبكة الألوان وضربات الفرشاة طبقة بعد أخرى. لكن هذا التغيير لم يكن باتجاه التوضيح التراكمي، فعلى حين غرة اختفت

ملامح الشبه الواضحة والناجحة بلا شك بسرعة وبدون سبب ظاهر مخلية الساحة لأوجه جديدة أو لفقدان الوجه بالكامل أحيانا. في غضون ذلك زاد التوتر، لم اعد أعرف ما إذا كان ذلك في الجلسة الثانية أو الثالثة عندما استبدل مروان فجأة قطعة القماش الصغيرة التي رسم عليها حتى ذلك الوقت بواحدة أكبر وبدأ جولة ثانية موازية. وبذلك دقت ساعة الجد في البحث عن الصورة. فبينما كان حتى الآن يعمل على تحديد معالم الرأس بدأ الآن في ترسيخ الشكل في اللوحة. وبما أنه تذكر أنه رآني مرة بصدرية زرقاء داكنة، جئت في المرة التالية مرتديا تلك الصدرية لأوفر له ذريعة لتثبيت رأسي على الكتفين، ولم أقص شعري أيضا حتى لا يظهر الرأس مغلقا ومعزولا على مساحة اللوحة.

ورغم كل شيء لم نصل إلى الختام مع هذه الصورة الثانية. القرار الدرامي الأخير تمثل في تلوين محيط رأسي بواسطة ريشة عريضة وبلون قرمزي شفاف له لمسة ماغينتا وهو اللون المميز لمروان.

كان ذلك المزيج الشبيه بالنبيذ الأحمر الساخن يمكن أن يكون فاتحة لجولة جديدة. لكن الظروف فرقتنا، فقد اضطررت لدخول المستشفى واضطر هو لمغادرة مرسمه العتيق المألوف. وهكذا لم أرَ الصورة الأولى الصغيرة مرة أخرى إلا قبل فترة وجيزة فتأكدت من كونها «شبيهة» جدا بالمفهوم الحديث المتطرف، فهي بالمفهوم التقليدي الدقيق ليست بورتريه تظهرني كفرد ولا تعكس صورة الجالس بأمانة. صحيح أن هناك ملامح أستطيع التعرف عليها على أنها لي: الرأس الكبير والنظرة غير المتوازية والمتهربة أو مجموعة قسمات الفم العريضة وغير الواضحة، لكن النسيج التصويري المتين لهذه المميزات لا يسمح بالتعرف على صاحبها وهو «أنا».

بل على العكس إذ تكشف صور مروان عن الغلالات الداخلية لموديلاته تلك الطبقات المتعددة التي يغطي بعضها بعض أجزاء البعض الآخر والتي تميز بمجموعها الكثافة الكاتمة لشخص ما وتقدم بذلك كاستثناءات نادرة في عمله دليلا هاما لفهم فنه على الإطلاق.

أما أنا فوجدت نفسي مصابا بدقة في هذا الحرمان من المعرفة البسيطة لذاتي. لقد جعلني شبيها بي، وإذا ما شئنا حل المقارنة مع أسطورة الملاكم محمد علي فيمكن القول: مروان ليس بطل الضربات القاضية ولا معلم الوخزات الصغيرة. استراتيجيته متميزة بحذاقة لا تقارن. فبالرقص بين الألوان على طاولة الرسم، والقماش على الحامل، ومنظري، ـ مُنقلاً بصره هنا وهناك ـ نسج خيوطه حولي وأسرني برقة ومكر حتى بدوت على قماشة الرسم بكل جلاء صورة حقيقية من إبداع مروان.

نقلها إلى العربية

حسين قره حمو– برلين.

عبد الرحمن منيف، ١٩٩٦.

زيت على قماش. ٧٠ x ٩٥ سم.

أدونيس
إشراقٌ في جسد المادّة

شيءٌ يَترحّلُ أبداً في بَيْداء اللاّشيء،
غيابٌ لكنْ لا يتلألأُ فيه غيرُ الحضور،
مادّةٌ كمثل الأثير تَنْسَبِكُ في خلايا ضوئيّة تسبح في شَبكة
الألوان حيث يتفتّتُ الضّوءُ ويتبعثر–منتظماً كأنه
نسيجٌ من خيوط ضباب تُوشّحه خيوط شَمسٍ سيريّةَ.

سمٌّ صُوفيٌّ يُخَلْخِلُ المادّة، لكنّه ليس إلا إكسيراً يبعث فيها
الحياة على نحوٍ آخر.

سماءٌ غير أنها بَشَرةٌ ثانية للأرض في ضوءٍ هو نفسه
لونٌ، في لونٍ يكاد أن يكون شكلاً، أو يكاد أن
يكون اليدَ الخفية التي ترسمُ الشكل.

ذلك ما أشعر به، ما أراه، في دَفْقٍ من
التضادّ، عندما أتأمّل في لوحات مروان.

حقّاً، يبدو لي مروان كمن يعمل على إرجاع الوجود
إلى طينه التكوينيَ الأول، والحياة إلى نبضها الجنينيَ
أو كمن يريد أن يخُضَّ الألوانَ ويرَجّهَا، مُحوّلاً إيّاها
إلى كائناتٍ لا نُرى منها إلا ظلالها.
في هذا وفيما وراءه،
أبدو لنفسي، أنا المشاهد، أمام لوحاتِه، أنّني أتمرأى
فيها، مقلّباً نظري في نهائيةٍ لا تتوقّفُ عن الصيرورة
وعن التقلُّب في صور من اللانهائية،
وفي وجوه غائمة كأنها أضواءٌ تحفّ بها ظلمات
العناصر، وتعجز عن أن تحجبها،

وفي ينابيع تخطُّ مجاريها كمثل أثلام على صفحة التراب.
وفي ضبابٍ يتمدّد غلائلَ شفافةً على قامة الأرض.
كأنني أمام طاقةٍ لا تتوقف عن توليد عالم يتَفَكَّك
ويتكوَّن في اللحظة نفسها:
يتفكَّك بفعل الحقيقة الوجودية،
ويتكوَّن بفعل المجاز الفنيّ.

هكذا،

بين نور يتغلغلُ في الظلمةِ اجتياحاً، حتى ليكاد أن
يطمسها مُهَيْمِناً عليها وعلى ما يحيط بها.
وظلمةٍ تسبحُ في النور حتى لتكاد أن تفيض متدفّقةً
من اللوحة، غامرةً كلَّ ما حولها!
تتحرّك الأشكال ثابتةً، وتثبت متحركةً في اندفاعٍ
كأنه إشراق في جسد المادة.
وكأنَّ اللوحة ليست مقيمةً في اللوحة،
وإنما هي طاقة إشعاع تتموج في فضاء النظر،
كما لو أنَّ المرئيّ هو، تحديداً، ما لا نراه

باريس، أول يناير ٢٠٠١

أدونيس، ٢٠٠١–٢٠٠٢.

زيت على قماش، ٨٩ × ١١٦ سم.